AMMA DARKO was born in Tamale, Ghana in 1956. She was brought up by adoptive parents in Accra. She studied at the University of Science and Technology at Kumasi, Ghana, graduating in 1980, and followed this with a year spent working for the Technology Consultancy Centre in Kumasi. After several years spent in Germany, where she had to take on menial work in order to survive, she returned to Ghana in 1987 to do a course in taxation. She is currently a tax inspector in Ghana. She is married and lives with her family in Tamale. *Beyond the Horizon* was originally written in English, but first published in Germany as *Der Verkaufte Traum* in 1991.

AMMA DARKO

BEYOND THE HORIZON

Heinemann

Heinemann Educational Publishers
A Division of Heinemann Publishers (Oxford) Ltd
Halley Court, Jordan Hill, Oxford OX2 8EJ

Heinemann: A Division of Reed Publishing (USA) Inc.
361 Hanover Street, Portsmouth, NH 03801–3912, USA

Heinemann Educational Books (Nigeria) Ltd
PMB 5205, Ibadan
Heinemann Educational Boleswa
PO Box 10103, Village Post Office, Gaborone, Botswana

FLORENCE   PRAGUE   PARIS   MADRID
ATHENS   MELBOURNE   JOHANNESBURG
AUCKLAND   SINGAPORE   TOKYO
CHICAGO   SAO PAULO

© Schmetterling Verlag GbR Paul Sandner & Jorg Hunger September 1991

First published as a German translation under the title *Der Verkaufte Traum*

First published in English by Heinemann Educational Publishers in 1995

British Library Cataloguing in Publication Data
A catalogue record for this book is available from the British Library.

Cover design by Touchpaper
Cover illustration by Alan Bond

ISBN 0435 90990 8

Phototypeset by CentraCet Limited, Cambridge
Printed and bound in Great Britain
by Cox & Wyman Ltd, Reading, Berkshire

95   96   97   98   11   10   9   8   7   6   5   4   3   2

1

I am sitting here before my large oval mirror. I like oval things. They are not too round and not too square, is what I say when people ask why my everything is oval, mirror, tables, all. Truth is, I just like ovals. I find them serene and they dispense more sympathy to me than other shapes. And God knows I need a bit of it.

I am staring painfully at an image. My image? No! – what is left of what once used to be my image. And from my left and right, all about me, I keep hearing chuckles and pantings, wild bedspring creaks, screaming oohs and yelling aahs. They are coming from rooms that are the same as mine, rooms where the same things are done as they are in mine. And in all of them there are pretty women like myself, one in each room waiting to be used and abused by strange men. They are all about me. And yet here by myself, alone inside my room, I feel so very, very far away on my own. So friendless, isolated and cold.

I am just in brief silky red underpants, so I'm virtually naked, but that is not why I feel so cold because this coldness I feel does not grip my body so much as it does my soul. It's deep inside me that feels this chilliness, from the dejected soul my body harbours, a soul grown old from too much use of its shelter. Yes! I've used myself and I have allowed myself to be too used to care any longer. But that doesn't render me emotionless. I've still got lots of feelings in me, though sometimes I'm not sure if they aren't the wrong ones.

Tears are building up in my eyes. They always do when I

1

stare at what is left of me. They are blurring my vision and are slowly rolling down my face in an agonising rhythm like the beating of the devil's own drums . . . ta . . . ta . . . ta . . . dropping down one after the other, painfully slow, painfully gradual, onto these two flabby, floppy drooping things I call my breasts, my tired graceless bosom. I fear what I see when I look at myself. I shiver at the sight of my sore cracked lips which still show through the multiple layers of the glossy crimson paint I apply to hide them. This gaudy pink rouge I've plastered on my ebony black face looks horrid too, I know, but I wear it because it's a trademark of my profession. What my poor mother back home in black Africa would say to these hideous traces of bites and scratches all over my neck, should she ever have the misfortune of seeing them, I fear to imagine. They extend even far beyond the back of my ears, several bruises and scars left generously there by the sadistic hands of my best payers, my best spenders. And even back down my spine too run a couple more – horrendous ones which I fortunately do not suffer the distaste of seeing vividly like those on my neck, and so I care less about them.

I have yet another handicap too, my little left finger. I think often of the games my mother used to play with them, my fingers. Childish games when I was her innocent naive child. 'Give me your hand,' she used to say. And I would give it to her. And she would take it, usually my left hand, and spread out my five fingers on her thighs, her coal-black thighs. And start the song: this one cries gaa gaa gaa, this one asks what is wrong, this one says maybe hunger, this one says let's go take and eat, but thicky Tom thumb won't agree, he says I'll tell when father comes, and so small goes crying on, gaa gaa gaa.

Small was my little finger and it still cries, but no more for mother's playful hunger. It's bent. Its bone's been displaced and it looks weird. I see it all the time and I loathe it, but not the money that came with it. The injury was done to me by one of my best spenders, a giant of a man but who always, when he comes to me, cries like a baby in my arms, telling me about his dictator wife whom he loves but who treats him so bad she makes him lick her feet at night. Then filled with the loathing and rage of revenge for this wife he'd love to kill, but lacking the guts even to pull her hair, he imagines me to be her, orders me to shout I am her, and does horrible things to me like I never saw a man ever do to a woman before in the bushes I hail from. But I bear it because it is part of my job. I listen attentively to his talk and comfort where I can. And even when he puts me in pain and spits upon me and calls me a nigger fool I still offer him my crimson smile and pretend he's just called me a princess, for I've got a job to do, and I've got to put my all in it. But like I said, I may be dirty, old and overused but I can still feel emotions. And that is why I cry sometimes. And when I've got my crying to do I sit here alone before my large oval mirror and stare painfully at this bit of garbage that once used to be me and I cry.

This room in which I am sitting is in a lone, isolated house on the outskirts of Munich, a house I hear once belonged to a prominent wealthy German who had it built for the purpose of his frequent clandestine rendezvous with the greatest love of his life who, like him, was a male. This led to his suicide when the truth about his sexuality emerged to the public. The house, following the tragedy, remained unoccupied for many years. Then a few years ago a man materialised from nowhere and bought the house with plenty cash and warned people to leave him alone. This man I call Oves. Formally, to others, he is Overseer. He is my lord, my master and my pimp. And like the other women on my left and right, I am his pawn, his slave and his property. What he orders, I do. It's my karma. Once, long ago, I believed mother when she said to me, 'Your life is your road, Mara. God puts you at the start of this road and propels you to walk on, and only He knows where your road will end, but it is the road He chose for you and you must walk it with gratefulness because it's the best for you.' Once, before I started to walk my road all on my own, I believed mother. But that was before I was given away to this man who paid two white cows, four healthy goats, four lengths of cloth, beads, gold jewellery and two bottles of London Dry Gin to my family, and took me off as his wife from my little African village, Naka, to him in the city.

I remember the day clearly. I returned from the village well

3

with my fourth bucket of water of the day when mother excitedly beckoned to me in all my wetness and muddiness, dragged me into her hut and breathlessly told me the 'good news'.

'Your father has found a husband for you,' she gasped, 'a good man!'

All I did was grin helplessly because I clearly remembered the same good news as this that mother had given my older sister two years before. Found, too, by father. And my sister was now a wreck. Naturally, not all husbands made wrecks of their wives. Many women in Naka were extremely content with their marriages and their husbands and wouldn't exchange them for anything in the world. And some such good men still existed in Naka. But father, it appeared, had a different formula for choosing or accepting husbands for his daughters, which took more into consideration the number of cows coming as the bride price than the character of the man.

'Who is he?' I asked mother, 'Father's choice for me?'

'Oh, dear child,' mother said, 'you know your father would consider it rude if I disclosed him to you before he did. Dress up,' she urged me, 'I am certain he will send for you soon.'

And he did. And made known to me that my chosen husband was the man named Akobi. And it astounded me, first, that this man had settled on me as his wife, and second, that father had had the guts to approach his father to offer him his daughter. But I soon learnt that, yes, Akobi chose me as his wife, but it was his father who had approached mine and not vice versa. And my astonishment was because of the position that Akobi's family held in the village.

Naka was a farming village, and Akobi's father, like most men in the village, was a farmer too. But unlike most men in the village, he was also an undertaker. And people feared him because he was a man who seldom issued threats but pitilessly carried out those he issued. A man who once shocked the entire village and beyond when he threatened to give the dying chief's linguist a 'banana funeral' because the old man owed him eight shillings and sixpence, and who, true to his word, presented the corpse on the funeral day wrapped in two large banana leaves. Unscrupulous though it was, it earned him great respect. And

4

when a nasty outbreak of cholera followed in the village, claiming the lives of many and increasing his income as the only under-taker, he earned even more respect for using the money to educate his son Akobi at the Joseph Father of Jesus Roman Catholic school, making his son the first child of Naka to earn a Form Four General Certificate. Of course, snide remarks were uttered that he was benefiting from the deaths of people, but who cared? The point was that his son had studied and got a certificate. They stood out in the village crowd and were held in high esteem.

But one thing Akobi's father did not reckon with was that his son would refuse to return to the village and farm with him. Akobi had other plans. He had tasted town life and was craving to further it to city life. And returning to Naka to become a farmer like all the rest who hadn't been to school at all, or even as undertaker like his father, was for him out of the question. Naturally, his father was very disappointed for he was looking forward to the help of the son he had invested so much in, but Akobi successfully convinced him of the urgency of his intentions, of how he wanted to get on in life which was by no means possible if he returned to live in the village. That was how, with his father's reluctant blessing, Akobi left Naka to go and live in the big city.

Life in the city, Akobi soon realised, was not the glamorous days and nights he had seen in his dreams. Reality hit him and hit him real hard, and he realised that the furthest he could go with his level of education was a messenger clerk at the Minis-tries, at best. But the worst confrontation of all for him were the women, one of whom he had hoped to make a wife and bring to Naka to pompously introduce. A typist or a secretary at the Ministries perhaps, who bathes with skin-bleaching soaps and applies skin-lightening creams, and who does wonders with hot combs and creams to her stubborn kinky hair to turn it long, straight and silky. It was a passionate dream Akobi soon realised he could never fulfil on his messenger clerk pay, since those kinds of women went out not with the likes of him but with bank managers, dubious businessmen and senior civil servants who could finance their requirements. Even accommodation, he soon realised, never came easy without the right amount of money in the pocket. And what accommodation the money in his pocket could afford, Akobi felt was too demeaning for someone like him with the kind of status he enjoyed in Naka.

So he was soon back in Naka to borrow money from his father who wasn't having it that rosy because no more fatal cholera had struck. He didn't come alone but with a pretty city woman who in pomp and style he introduced as a special friend he had brought along to show the beauties of Naka. Comfort was her name, a typist at the Ministries, and the truth was that Akobi was hoping that witnessing at first-hand the high esteem he enjoyed in the village would impress Comfort and get her uttering a breathless 'Yes' when later he proposed love to her. But it was a miscalculation. A sad one, for Comfort's admiration ended abruptly the moment they left the boundaries of Naka. And the very next day, back within the walls of the Ministries, Comfort gave him a nasty cold shoulder. Ignoring him, she elegantly disappeared into the back of the silver metallic Pontiac belonging to the ugly, fat First Secretary to the Housing and Construction Minister, who in spite of his munched-up face and flabby pot belly had laid half the pretty girls about and who still continues to lay them, the likes of Comfort, in exchange for empty promises of a bungalow and a Morris Minor. This snub was the last straw for Akobi. The money he went borrowing from his father, he saved, and he set about searching for cheap accommodation compatible with his pocket. Several weeks later, with his heart torn in two, he showed up unexpectedly in Naka, impressively clad in pencil-striped grey trousers, a stiffly starched and ironed white shirt, a thin black tie, and impeccably polished black Beatles boots, and announced to his father in all earnestness his ardent desire for a wife from the village.

I don't know why of all the eligible women in the village his father chose me. I only know that the choice, for my father, could not have come at a better time. A man he owed money to had come and forcefully claimed his debt in the form of eight of father's eleven goats. So my dowry came in handy. And then, too, he was flattered that the first Naka son with a school certificate should choose his daughter for a wife. So much so that

I later learnt that, drunk from palmwine and belching boisterously, he had proclaimed that he would gladly have given me
away even for one goat. But like I said, Akobi's father bought me
off very handsomely. And while Akobi returned to the city to
work, the customs and traditional rites were got over and done
with on his behalf. Three weeks later he came straight from work
on a Friday evening, arriving in Naka on Saturday, and left for
the city on the same Saturday with me as his wife ... and
property!

2

To say I was shocked when Akobi brought me to his home in the
city would be an understatement. I was stunned. Our homes in
the village were of mud and leaves but no one needed to tell a
visitor they were homes. Akobi had to tell me this was his home
before I believed it. First, there wasn't the group of huts with
large compounds about them and backyard gardens that I was
used to in the village, but a cluster of shabbily-constructed
corrugated-iron sheet shelters that looked like chicken houses,
while all about and between them shallow, open gutters wound
their way. In these gutters, due to the lack of any drainage
system, all the water from dirty washing and bathing, and urine
too, collected and stayed until it evaporated. And since the rate
of evaporation was slower than the rate at which the waste waters
collected, the resulting standing water not only stank but also
bred nasty shades of algae and generations of large fat mosquitoes
that greedily fed on our blood at night. As if that wasn't enough,
barely fifty yards away there was an unhygienic public toilet
beside which was the area's only public rubbish dump. I was
soon to learn that the rubbish was collected only once every two
months or so. And so this also not only brought in swarms of
flies in their thousands but polluted the surrounding air so
intensely that one hardly ever woke up in the morning without
either a splitting headache or a bleeding nose. The situation was
utterly depressing, the more so because I had yet to make friends
with the occupants of the other shelters. And even though the
thought of returning to the village crossed my mind, I knew it

was something I could never do. Not only would I not be welcomed back into the family, but father would never be able to afford to refund my dowry, much of which he'd already squandered. So, come what may, I was stuck with the flies and the blood-sucking war the mosquitoes had declared on us. I was soon to discover that these would not be my only headache.

Parts of the corrugated-iron-sheet shelters had rusted away and left little holes here and there which, though too small for the heads of humans to pass through, were large enough for inquisitive mice and other creatures to slip through. Lift a pan here and out would jump a toad. Pull a chair there to sweep behind it and what should dash feverishly past but a bright orange-headed lizard. Spiders, wasps and cockroaches were all about. So here and there I sealed with broken pieces of bricks and clay and anything that could seal, even wet bread and corn dough. But those were just the holes I saw.

Then came the rainy season and with it my first conflict with the landlord, Alhaji. Eccentric as he was, he had strongly forbidden any tenant to carry out any form of repair work on his 'houses'. Anyone who disobeyed him risked eviction. He was a self-styled renovator, carrying out all repair work by himself and charging his tenants for his labour. As it was an extra source of finance he wasn't going to let anyone off. And there existed stark evidence that he did the job badly most times just so that the repair wouldn't last very long, to create yet another opportunity for him to enforce his labour. So it was only repair works inside the room where I was not likely to be seen or caught by Alhaji, that I carried out myself. As for all the others, like the leaks from the roof, I had to wait until Alhaji had time or inclination to carry them out himself.

Our room itself was just large enough for Akobi's dried-grass mattress, an old three-legged centre-table whose missing fourth leg had been substituted by a high pile of cement brick pieces, and an armchair. In one corner was Akobi's one and only portmanteau and my one and only wicker basket that served as my portmanteau. From one corner to the opposite corner was a short drying line on which Akobi always hung his grey trousers, white shirt and black tie that constituted his daily office wear, while below it his Beatles boots found their resting place. They were his pride.

I made my first friend after about six weeks. Mama Kiosk was what people called her because she owned a kiosk at the main lorry station in which she retailed cigarettes, sweets and iced water. Her home was not Alhaji's but her own. It wasn't all corrugated-iron sheets but part blocks. I was going to throw my rubbish away one day when I heard from behind me, 'Hey woman! Hey, hey, greenhorn!' I turned. I didn't know that greenhorn was something rude until, laughing, she said she only meant it as a joke. 'You are the new tenant here?' she asked.

'Yes,' I replied.

'You come from the village? Johnnie-just-come? Villager-in-town?'

'Yes.'

'And that Ministries man with the big flat nose, is that your husband?'

'Yes.'

She laughed, sized me up and down, then asked, 'Do you work?'

'No,' I replied, 'but I am hoping to find something to do soon.'

'You want work? Now?'

'Yes, if there is work . . . now.'

'Are you going to the rubbish dump?'

'Yes,' I replied.

'Can you take mine with you? I never find the time for it, you know. And my daughters don't, either.'

'Yes,' I said, and took her rubbish with mine to the dump.

She was standing where I left her when I returned. I gave her her garbage can and turned to go.

'Hey,' she called, surprised, 'you are truly a greenhorn, you know.'

I stood staring at her.

'Hey, do you work for free in the village?' she asked derisively. But I still could not get what she was hinting at and continued to stare at her.

'You are in the city,' she said emphatically, 'and in the city nothing is for free, you get me? Come!' She beckoned, and I followed her into her house. Minutes later, I emerged with a paper bag filled with a piece of yam, two cassavas, some okros and a handful of garden eggs. 'For throwing my rubbish away for me,' she added at the door. I thanked her warmly and left.

When Akobi returned I told him. While I wasn't expecting him to go tango dancing in gratitude at Mama Kiosk's door, neither did I expect him to sneer and call me a dirty village beggar. Yet the following morning he told me to my face that since I had got food for the day he might as well save his chop money.

For a while after I didn't go throwing Mama Kiosk's rubbish away for her, until one Saturday afternoon when Akobi had left to go and meet friends for an outing, which he always did without me, and Mama Kiosk called me and asked if I would throw her rubbish away for her for a few fingers of plantain. I said I couldn't because my husband didn't like it, and left her standing there.

Akobi returned home that night just after midnight. Though I heard him I continued to feign a deep sleep, when suddenly I felt a painful kick in my ribs. Astounded to the point of foolishness, I jumped up in confusion. What had I done? He had never kicked nor slapped me before so what was wrong? He wasn't drunk. Before I could ask what I had done, he bellowed angrily, 'You foolish lazy idiot! What do you think you are sitting here all day doing nothing and yet refusing to work for Mama Kiosk. You think here is a pension house?'

I stared at him. 'I refused to work for Mama Kiosk?' I asked.

'Shut up!' he roared, landing me a slap on one cheek. I scurried into one corner and slumped on the floor, my burning face buried in my hands. I understood the world no more.

'Now listen to me,' he resumed, 'from now on you will throw Mama Kiosk's rubbish away for her and she will pay you with foodstuffs and vegetables. And since that means you need not go to the market often, I can also save by cutting down on the daily chop money I give you, you understand?'

'Yes,' I replied, shaking all over.

'And sleep on your mat today. I want to sleep on the mattress alone,' he added. He hopped into bed. Seconds later, he was

11

snoring away. I lay there on the mat spread on the hard floor, trying to tolerate the mice and cockroaches, my eyes wide open. I lay there like that until the first rays of the morning sunlight streamed through.

I didn't see Mama Kiosk again till Monday morning and confronted her with, 'Why did you lie to my husband?'

'I lied to your husband?' Mama Kiosk was astonished, mainly because, as she later said, she never imagined that I was capable of getting angry, and secondly, because she hadn't lied to Akobi. I showed her my swollen cheek and told her the story. I must say she was really drained at the end of it.

'I never told your husband that you were refusing to work for me,' she said. 'I met him Saturday night at Lido Club and just asked why he got angry that you threw my rubbish away for me. He laughed and said he would put it right. That was all. But that he would come and beat and kick you in the night for it, I never imagined that that's what he meant. Never.'

I saw how bad Mama Kiosk felt about the matter and suggested that she bother her head no more about it, that we left it as it was and I would resume throwing her rubbish away for her. So with this arrangement a close relationship between Mama Kiosk and me began.

Initially, many things that happened in my marriage appeared to me to be matter-of-course things that happened in all marriages and to all wives. I didn't see much difference from my parents' marriage either, so why should I think differently just because I was living in the city? For instance, it was natural that after I had woken up first at dawn, and made the fire to warm up water for Akobi, and carried a bucketful of it with his spongebag to the public bathhouse for him, and returned to wake him up to tell him his bath was ready – it was natural that I also had to stand outside while he bathed just in case some soap suds should go into his eyes and he should need me. Moreover, it was me who always carried back the empty bucket and the bathing accessories and saw to drying his towel ready for next morning since he hated wet towels touching his skin. It was natural, too, that when he demanded it, I slept on the concrete floor on just my thin mat while he slept all alone on the large grass mattress since, after all, mother had taught me that a wife was there for a man for one thing, and that was to ensure his well-being, which included his pleasure. And if demands like that were what would give him pleasure, even if just momentarily, then it was my duty as his wife to fulfil them. So that even those nights when he ordered me to sleep on the thin mat on the hard floor, even if I laid there and could not sleep and suffered a splitting headache the next day because of lack of sleep, I still regarded my suffering as part of being a wife, and endured it just like I would menstrual pain. That he had bought me no new clothes and left me still with only those I had come in from the village, and that in spite of this he had also forbidden me to sew any of the cloth he had presented me with as part of my dowry, I saw also as falling under 'obey and worship your husband', as my parents and family elders stringently repeated to me at the end of the marriage rites. In other words, that, too, was for me normal.

But all these things that I considered to be normal, Mama Kiosk did not find normal. 'Your husband is one of those men who have no respect for village people,' she said once. 'Tradition demands that the wife respect, obey and worship her husband but it demands, in return, care, good care of the wife. Your husband neglects you and yet demands respect and complete worship from you. That is not normal.' And the closer our relationship became, the more effort she made to let me see and understand that my husband was not treating me right. But I saw none of it, or maybe I simply lacked the ability to understand it enough to see.

'Hey, I have seen your Ministries man in a new embroidery shirt,' she said once.

'Yes, he bought it yesterday. Isn't it beautiful?' I replied with pride.

'And what did he buy for you?' Mama Kiosk asked.

'Nothing,' I replied. 'Should he have?'

'Tell me,' retorted Mama Kiosk, 'you find it normal that he buys for himself and buys nothing for you?'

'Because he is the man,' I answered.

'Because he is a man, but a bad husband,' Mama Kiosk snapped. 'Men buy for themselves, Mara. There's no law that

13

says they shouldn't. But they buy for their wives too, Mara. And there's a law that says they must. You have never peeled these clothes off since you came here, except on Saturdays to wash them. And you call that normal?'

I must say that Mama Kiosk nearly convinced me at this point because even though it was true that I saw my mother worship my father daily, I saw, too, that father took ample care of her. Her clothes, at least, were never dirty. And she had more than one outfit. Indeed, she had plenty. But still I wasn't going to let Mama Kiosk spoil my marriage for me, so I said, 'Mama Kiosk, I probably have eyes that see blue where you see red. But I would still not like to exchange my eyes for yours. I like my eyes as they are.'

This remark Mama Kiosk took to heart. And for a long time she completely suspended her preachings. She still continued sometimes to call me greenhorn, but no longer with the same implication as at first. She intoned it more playfully and always accompanied it with a laugh.

3

Three months passed. Then one day I went and knocked on Mama Kiosk's door. She let me in, calling jovially, 'Greenhorn, what brings you here at this hour?'

'There is something wrong with me, Mama Kiosk,' I uttered under my breath, 'and I must talk to somebody.'

Her jovial look turned serious. 'Come,' she beckoned me to a seat, and added, 'you have something serious on your chest, I can see. Let it out. Mama Kiosk's ears are all wide for you, Mara.' And so I got underway.

'I haven't seen my blood for two months now, Mama Kiosk,' I began, 'and I am also suffering fits and dizziness. You think I'm dying?'

To my astonishment, Mama Kiosk roared with laughter, stood me up on my feet, clasped me to her generous bosom, and shrieked excitedly, 'You are pregnant, greenhorn! You are carrying a baby!' Then she drew me back, looked lovingly upon my face and resumed, 'Your Ministries man will be proud of you, Mara. Bet my neck. Men like him feel great when they see the results of their handiwork. I am sure that from now on he won't forget so easily that you too have feelings. He will acknowledge your existence and start treating you well.'

But somehow I couldn't bring myself to share Mama Kiosk's enthusiasm. It was fine that I was going to have a baby. At least it would prove to the world that I was fertile and bring honour to my family. But as to whether that would automatically mean Akobi would stop beating me, buy me some new clothes and

15

resume giving me chop money regularly instead of making me throw people's rubbish away for them in return for food, I wasn't so convinced. I did see all these things as normal, as I have said, but it didn't mean that I liked them. It was just like my menstrual pains. It was a natural thing but it didn't mean that I liked it. I would have wished that it wasn't there, just like Akobi's bad treatment of me, but the very thought of the non-existence of both always filled me with fear. For me, not obeying and worshipping Akobi would make me less of a wife, just as having no menstrual periods would make me less of a woman. And I didn't want to be less of anything.

My family and Akobi's family back in the village, I knew, would also share in the joy of my pregnancy. But unlike Mama Kiosk, I wasn't so certain that Akobi would be pleased. The first time he slept with me, when he started moving quicker and panting louder and sweating more, he suddenly at one stage removed himself very quickly from inside me and wetted me all over with this strange milky-white liquid coming from his manhood. At first I thought that he was sick and was throwing up through his manhood. But then he told me that it was to avoid something. I wanted to tell Mama Kiosk all this and ask if it wasn't making a baby that Akobi wanted to avoid since, after this first time, it became something he always did when he slept with me, but I felt a bit embrarrassed about telling Mama Kiosk all this and so said simply, 'Let's wait and see.' And we saw.

'Akobi,' I called softly after supper next day when I thought he was in a relatively good mood, 'I was by Mama Kiosk today and I told her that I haven't had my blood for two months and she says I am by all means carrying a baby.'

I had just given him a piece of chewing stick when I started, and he was removing bits from his teeth; but now he stopped dead, the stick still stuck somewhere between two of his upper teeth. Then slowly he removed the stick, sucked through his teeth and said, 'Mama Kiosk says you are pregnant?'

'Yes, Akobi,' I answered. And sat on the chair because I felt a sudden dizziness.

'Did Mama Kiosk sleep with you?' he asked, still in that disregarding tone. I felt a cold sweat seep through my pores. I didn't answer. Then suddenly there was this angry roar of, 'Get up!' like an over-irritated boar and the next second I was up at attention on my two feet. I didn't know which I was most, scared, angry or perplexed. He studied me like he was studying filth. My instincts had been right all along. His father might want ten grandchildren as he had said the day they presented the dowry to my family, but his son obviously didn't. He took his eyes off me. I remained standing. Then, ignoring me, he resumed cleaning his teeth and sucking through them. Then, staring straight ahead of him as if looking into a crystal ball, he asked almost absent-mindedly, 'And why did you get pregnant?'

I thought: I couldn't have heard right. 'Pardon?' I replied spontaneously, and before I knew what was happening . . . Wham! first slap . . . wham! wham! wham! three more in succession. And I scurried into what had now become my favourite corner, slumping to the floor. What had I done wrong? But I was to be given neither reasons nor explanations. He stormed out of the room and didn't come back again until late at night. I was sleeping on the mat on the floor. I didn't dare to sleep on the mattress. He stumbled into the room and went straight to bed. For the next two days he spoke no word to me. Mama Kiosk was totally flabbergasted when I told it all to her. What African man got angry because his wife was carrying a baby? And the first baby at that.

'Mara,' began Mama Kiosk, 'this your Ministries man, he is not only a bad man and a bad husband, he has also got something inside his head. I only hope that he won't destroy you with it before you too start seeing red with your eyes like I do.'

The third day he spoke with me. 'I have decided that you must start work to earn proper money, now that we are going to increase,' he began. 'You have been here long enough now, and you can work. I can't cater for us all when your child comes' (the 'your' didn't escape me), 'and I have more important plans.'

'Yes, Akobi,' I replied.

So I started looking for work in addition to keeping home, earning foodstuffs with my rubbish dumpings, serving him still to the full which meant still being the first to get up mornings to make fire and warm water for him and stand by while he bathed,

17

and of course also carrying the bucket of water daily to the bathroom for him in spite of my physical change. And I dared not ask questions or make demands.

It was Mama Kiosk who suggested that I should take up hawking boiled eggs to travellers at the lorry station where she had her kiosk because it was a very popular snack with them. And when in the end no better alternative cropped up, I went to Akobi with this hint. He agreed that it was worth a try, and gave me the capital for my first batch of eggs plus the sieve container in which the land law required cooked foods to be sold, but not before he had made it clear to me that he expected me to repay the capital as soon as I had made my first profits. And to blackmail me mentally into keeping my word, knowing how superstitious I was, he made me swear to the river god to drown me if I didn't. Two days later, I left for the first time with Mama Kiosk to begin my trade.

I never imagined it to be such a brisk trade as it turned out to be. Neither did I consider that trading this way would be so exciting. The lorry station was a place of colour. The people in their various coloured up-and-down clothes and headties. The kiosks. Mama Kiosk's kiosk was blue. Others were yellow and some even orange. And then the lorries and trucks with their colours and inscriptions at the front and the back: DON'T LIE SON LEST YOUR MAMA LAY YOU. And another, LIFE IS WHAT YOU MAKE IT. The one that usually parked where I rested had for instance: GOD WILL SHOW ... IF YOU SHOW, while behind it another had: WHO IS HE ... HE IS SHE! I soon learnt that the owner of this truck had an arch-rival who was impotent and he deliberately taunted him with this fact.

To cut a long story short, I began enjoying my trade very much and daily thanked Akobi in my head that he made me start work at all. My eggs, too, were going so fast that by the second week I had doubled the quantity I took for sale. But then it meant that the more eggs I cooked to sell, the longer I stayed on at the station. And the longer I stayed on at the station, the later I got with getting Akobi's supper ready. Akobi hated to come home and be faced with the prospect of having to wait a couple of minutes longer than usual for his supper. Initially, he used only to grumble to show his disapproval, then when that still did not bring a change he began to act. When I didn't bring him the bowl of water and soap in time for washing his hands before and after eating, I received a nasty kick in the knee. When I forgot the chewing stick for his teeth, which he always demanded be placed neatly beside his bowl of served food, I got a slap in the face. And when the napkin was not at hand when he howled for it, I received a knuckle knock on my forehead. Then one afternoon it rained when I was half-way home, so that by the time I arrived home his towel, which I had left hanging outside, was completely soaked. And because it continued to rain throughout the night the towel didn't dry. This had never happened before. Before I had started working I had always been at home when the rain appeared to be wanting to fall. He had only one towel and like I said, he passionately hated wet towels.

I stood by as usual as he bathed that morning, having simply hung the towel in the bathroom for him, too afraid to inform him beforehand that it was wet. That he was intending something with me I saw at once when, having finished bathing, he emerged from the bathroom holding the empty bucket in which were his sponge bag and towel, instead of leaving it for me to pick up. I stood there, waiting for the doom I knew was coming. My fate. And he stopped right before me, bucket in left hand, a dead serious look on his face. For a moment I thought that he was just intending me to disappear into mother earth, under his withering look, maybe to force open the earth under my feet and bury myself inside it for good. But he had a more realistic plan. Just when I least expected it, he grabbed my left ear between his thumb and forefinger and, with my body slanted halfway towards him, my ears burning hot in pain, walked slowly and steadily with me back into our room. By the time he released me my left ear had gone numb. He said nothing more. He didn't even touch me again. He just left the next decision to me. And I took it without delay. I cut down on my daily quantity of eggs just to be home in time to attend to his wishes.

I was always calculating my money to see when I could pay Akobi back his capital and still be left with something after I had also deducted the cost of my next quantity of eggs. And this goal I reached after eleven weeks. Akobi had not touched me again since that drag by the ear but he wasn't treating me that kindly either. So I was happy when I finally counted out his capital, rolled the notes and neatly tied them with a string and proudly awaited his arrival to present the bundle to him. He came home that day with a friend, another messenger clerk at the Ministries who was about the only co-worker who knew where Akobi lived. This was because Yopi, as they called him, I don't know why, also lived in a shabby place just like we did and thus could not laugh at Akobi about it. But even then Akobi had issued this order to me to always keep clear when he returned home with Yopi. So though Yopi knew I was Akobi's wife, he had only seen me at a distance. But what did it matter? The point was that Akobi was always cheerful when he came home with Yopi. And even after Yopi had left he was usually decent to me. So I thought that today in his good mood when Yopi was gone I would also add to his jolliness by surprising him with his neatly rolled capital. And I must say too that I had this secret burning hope that the situation might mark a turning point in our marriage. So, late evening, when he was sitting before our door, seemingly in deep thought as I had often seen him, I approached him with the money. He didn't take it immediately. He smiled, just smiled, then got up wordlessly and led the way into the room, carefully closing the door behind him. I smiled too inside my head because when Akobi closed the door on the two of us in the room, one of two things happened. He either beat me or slept with me. I smiled in my head because I was utterly convinced that today it was going to be the latter, considering too that he hadn't touched me since knowing that I was pregnant.

We were in there alone now and the air about us was heavy. Then he turned and faced me and studied me briefly, cynically; and I sweated my first sweats of doubt. Then he snatched the money from me, counted and re-counted it, God knows how many times, then to my utter astonishment, slapped me hard across the face. I was stunned. I mean, Akobi was not beating me for the first time and this was not going to be the last beating, but most times in the past I had expected the beating, or even if

20

I hadn't expected it, I hadn't expected love either. This day not only did I not expect any beating, I also expected love. So this slap with its shock pain hurt me more than ever. I was so totally flabbergasted for I didn't know what it was I had done wrong or indeed if I had done anything wrong. I stared back at him, perplexed, and in doubt as to whether I would ever learn what angers Akobi and what doesn't. I just didn't know him. I was living with this man and sleeping in one room with him and I just didn't know him. I stared down at my belly. It clearly protruded now. I placed my two hands on it as though I was afraid the baby would slip out dead from between my thighs any moment. And for the first time ever I felt not just the physical pain but an intense emotional one too. My hand was still on my belly and I felt the baby move. I had felt its movements a couple of times already in the past few days but this was the first time that I felt it move with my hand on this belly of mine that was containing it. And it was a moment I would have loved to share with Akobi. But Akobi was a closed man; no one saw inside him. At least I didn't. But I dearly wished there, that moment, that somehow he too could feel it, the movement in my belly, for maybe it would have revived his human instincts.

'What do you mean paying without interest?' he bellowed eventually.

I didn't know what interest was so asked meekly, 'What?' And at the same instant I saw his clenched knuckles ready to knock pain into my forehead. I don't know what made me do what I did, but suddenly I wasn't prepared to take any more of it. I didn't wait to think. I rushed out of the room screaming, my extended belly leading me, and headed straight to Mama Kiosk. Mama Kiosk took me in, gave me cold water to drink and settled me down on her old sofa. As for me, yet again I simply did not understand the world any more. Outside, people were gathering and grouping in the compound. They were talking and gossiping their hearts out but I didn't care. Indeed I liked it because it was my screams that brought them out and very soon they were all going to learn the one thing I wanted them to know, that Akobi maltreated me. How Akobi was feeling too I could guess. I knew for sure that if he had known that I was going to take this action he wouldn't have done what he did, for he was a man who craved recognition as a civilised person and a gentleman, whatever that meant, and as the saying went in the city, only bushmen beat their wives. I felt good just thinking how terrible he must be feeling.

He didn't come after me but I wasn't going to spend too long a time at Mama Kiosk's lest I abuse her hospitality, so I left after about an hour but with the determination that if he ever touched me again I would leave the house. Not back to Mama Kiosk's but to the next place my eyes would set sight upon and I didn't care if it was the top of the rubbish dump. But it didn't come to that. He was lying on the mattress, face up, looking thoughtfully at the ceiling when I entered. Cool, composed and authoritative, he indicated with a pat of his hand on the space beside him that I should lie down beside him. I did so, more out of apprehension of starting another fight than anything else. Wordlessly, he stripped off my clothes, stripped off his trousers, turned my back to him and entered me. Then he ordered me off the mattress to go and lay out my mat because he wanted to sleep alone.

4

Between Mama Kiosk and me now existed a mother–daughter relationship. I had grown to trust her and to talk openly with her about everything. Then too she was the one person I spent most of my time with since I left in the morning with her to go to the station and returned in the evening with her. But probably what drew me even closer to her was that though I was well advanced in my pregnancy Akobi still wouldn't let me inform my people back in the village about it. He didn't tell me why but he didn't need to because I knew. He feared that my mother would probably propose to come and live with us until after my child was born and thus see at first hand for herself how wretchedly we lived, something he knew would not go down too well. So it was that in my desperate need for a mother I saw a substitute in Mama Kiosk. And she took on the role wholeheartedly, advising me on what to do and what not to do; asking and searching for herbs, which she made me sniff and chew; bringing me up to date on hygiene and noting down for me things I could start buying. She was a true friend and a perfect substitute mother. And I valued her enormously. But not so, Akobi. Apart from a couple more knocks on my forehead he had in general stopped beating me, but he didn't like it that I was growing more and more emotionally dependent on Mama Kiosk. He had observed that I had resumed singing when I was cooking or washing; and he didn't like it. I had become more liberal in my approach to the other tenants and turned into more of a conversationalist who now had various things in common with

23

them to talk about: trade, people, pregnancy, babies; and he didn't like it.

I wasn't taking money from him for our daily meals again. I had bought myself a pair of car-tyre slippers and Mama Kiosk had presented me with an old set of clothes which I was now alternating weekly with my own old one. I was still throwing away people's rubbish for them twice a week but this time, as Mama Kiosk would say, no one does nothing for free in the city. I wasn't waiting for them to pay me with just any foodstuffs but was demanding specific ingredients that went into making my full meals without me having to do extra shopping. Yam from here, plantain from there, garden-eggs and pepper from here, tomatoes and smoked fish from there; and I had my full meal for the day and even extra for the next morning. This my growing self-confidence Akobi didn't like either. In his search for answers he sought somewhere to put the blame. Not surprisingly he landed on Mama Kiosk.

'Mara,' he called me one afternoon, 'from now on I don't want you to leave in the mornings for the station together with Mama Kiosk. I protested feebly, 'Why?'

'Because I say so,' he replied with a cool defiance, 'and who taught you to put whys to my orders?'

Anxious to avoid another quarrel, I replied weakly, 'All right,' and in the night sneaked out and went and informed Mama Kiosk about it.

I knew Mama Kiosk would have wished to confront Akobi about it. And I knew too that many times in the past she had wished she could do so about one thing or the other. But since that first confrontation with Akobi in the early days of my living there, which had resulted in my first beating, she had set herself against poking her nose into our affairs, as she put it. So she wished me luck and said not to worry. 'We will meet daily at the station, anyhow. That one he can't prevent,' she added.

Then came next morning and for the first time Mama Kiosk and I left separately for the bus stop from which we daily rode on one of the intercity trucks to the main station, just like Akobi demanded. And yet we found ourselves riding on the same truck as in the past because we both arrived at the bus stop within

24

seconds of each other. In other words, it was just like old times, as though we had left the house together. This Akobi found out, and acknowledged that even if he banned me from leaving the house together with Mama Kiosk in the mornings, we would still end up on the same truck to the station. So that evening when he returned from work he went a step further with the issue of another order.

I used to leave the house each morning before he did. Now, said he, I was no longer to leave before him. I was to wait and leave together with him. This would ensure that I didn't go on the truck with Mama Kiosk.

'All right, Akobi,' I nodded submissively. Next morning I left later with him, he smart in his pencil-striped grey trousers, snow-white shirt, thin black tie and sharply pointed Beatles boots, with me beside him in my old faded clothes, my crude thick-soled rubber-tyre slippers and on my head, my sieve container full of cooked eggs.

I don't think that all this while that we had been living together Akobi had really bothered to take a close look at me in my shabby clothes concealing this extended belly of mine. But that morning he did. And from the look on his face at the bus stop as I waited for my truck and he for his Ministries bus, he didn't like what he saw. And to make matters worse, his bus arrived filled with 'gentlemen and ladies' co-workers like himself who saw that he knew me. I don't know what went on in the bus or at the work place but something must have happened because, following this first day, his attitude changed at the station. He was still unwilling to let me leave with Mama Kiosk, so he would leave with me, but at the station he left a respectable space between us. Then, too, about the time his bus usually arrived he would stretch his neck to see from afar if it was coming. And when he saw it coming he would very quickly and hastily move even farther away from me as if suddenly I was a stink-bomb scheduled to go off soon. When the bus stopped, unlike the first day when he muttered a curt 'Bye', he would board it without a look or glance at me. I wasn't as naive as before. I knew he was desperately trying to give the impression that he didn't know me. Above all, he didn't want the people in the bus to know that I

25

was his wife., Those males who like him were all in pencil-striped trousers, white shirts, thin ties and Beatles boots, and their females who all glittered in their painted faces, their screaming red lips and their gleaming straightened hair: that was his world, and I, with my old clothes, kinky hair and old tyre-slippers, didn't belong in it.

A couple of days later something I had never really given much thought to began to happen. I began to miss Mama Kiosk really badly. We still saw each other at the station, but between her trading and my hawking we had very little time to talk, something we used to do in the mornings on our way to the bus station and on the truck to the station. And in the evenings, too, since I had cut down on my eggs to arrive home early to prepare Akobi's supper, it wasn't always that we found ourselves returning home at the same time and on the same truck. It was this inner loneliness that made me summon all the God-given courage I had in me and ask Akobi why he still wanted to leave home with me if he was so ashamed of me at the bus stop. To my amazement, he was surprised not only that I should have asked at all but also that I seemed not to be seeing it as the most natural matter-of-course thing he should do. 'Don't you know that if they find out that I know you they will laugh at me?' So I took it that so must it be even though I didn't agree with it. And I would have learnt to live in peace with the fact just as I had done with so many other things. I would be Akobi's hidden wife, so that harmony would prevail in the marriage, something I saw as my duty and my responsibility as the wife to ensure. But fate, it seemed, had other plans because it did not wish it so.

I found out through someone's careless talk that the other hawkers had nicknamed me Boneshaker, which was also the nickname of the large passenger lorries because of the way the passengers travelling in them felt their bones rattle inside them as the lorry bumped in and out of the many pot holes that characterised almost all roads in the country. This name was thought suitable for me owing to my slippers which were made from the abandoned tyres of these lorries.

I was very pregnant then and had turned intolerant, so that on hearing this the anger welled up in me and I had a nasty fight with the station's most acclaimed chief gossip, Esiama, a large-bosomed lover of the boss of the truck drivers, after I had been told that it was she who had spitefully said, 'Ah! God forbid! But I will rather go barefooted than wear slippers like that!'

Actually I don't know where I got the strength for the fight considering my pregnancy. But when I started to fight with her I think I saw her as an enemy that was part Esiama, part Akobi and part my father. And the deep deep inner loathing I felt for all three transformed into such fearlessness and aggression that I took on this Esiama woman with a might I never thought I possessed. I beat her so well that as I later heard I left her with two of her front teeth missing, poor woman. 'My teeth, my teeth!' they say she went on screaming as she scrambled on her knees, her hands aggressively searching the hot sand for them as though if she found them she could stick them back in place in her gum like a contact lens in the eye. I received all the cheers; I deserved it. I got all the praises as the mighty one; that too I earned. Still, the consequences of my action lurked in the background awaiting the right moment to rear their head. And this came the very next day.

Esiama's lover, the drivers' boss, ordered his people not to pick up any passengers who bought eggs from me. Since people desperately wanting to travel always far outnumbered the trucks and lorries available, the passengers also fell in with this ban, for no one was going to sacrifice an urgent trip for my boiled eggs. So on the first boycott day I found myself stuck with all my cooked eggs. I only succeeded in getting rid of them later on at the night market and at a drastically reduced price. When this continued for the next two days I told Akobi about it and that I couldn't go on selling eggs at the station. I thought for a moment that he was going to die because his face turned at once ashen grey. It was like he was suddenly having problems breathing. I soon found out that it was no heart or brain attack as I had feared but rage, hell-red rage. He howled, growled and bawled. If I thought he was going to resume giving me money for our daily meals, he snarled, then I was kidding myself. He had more important plans for his money, he went on, and no way was he prepared to hear again that I wasn't going to trade any more, unless I was willing to wake up dead next day. Of course I didn't know how one could wake up dead, but the anger I saw had possessed him could have made me believe anything, so I promised him in desperation that I would soon find something else to do. Even that failed to cool him down and, as he continued raging, I began even to fear that yes, maybe there was a mysterious way after all that could leave me waking up dead next day. I made up my mind.

Mama Kiosk had given me a herb that, when I chewed just one leaf, made me sleep soundly. Next day when Akobi returned from work I served him an appetising spinach and crab soup with snails, smoked fish and pig's feet swimming exotically in it. The smile on his face when I set it down before him is not easy to forget. And he feasted upon it gleefully. Within the hour he was in a deep sleep.

I packed what I could into my wicker basket and left the room for the bus stop. Minutes later I got on a bus that took me to the station. An hour and a half later I was on a Boneshaker on route to Naka.

I arrived in the village next day but met with very little sympathy, as I had always feared. My father was not even interested to see me because he had taken on yet another wife, a young hot-blooded widow who had so filled his head that mother even cried to me that she was certain that their youngest rival had done ju-ju on father to cause him to forget and disregard his other wives. And so convinced was she that she had even been to the medicine man to ask him to perform a counter ju-ju and as a result was wearing heavy waist-beads of cowries and dried bones. My sisters too did not understand why I had fought with Esiama at all in the first place. If she had laughed at my slippers, so what? they queried. My expectations had grown high, they accused. In the village I went barefoot so a pair of tyre slippers, even crude ones, was a luxury that should never have been a cause for a fight. Not even if I was laughed at. So seeing the situation as it was, I abandoned the idea of announcing my wish that the marriage be dissolved, something I had been intending since I considered that the goats and cows presented for my dowry had probably by now given birth to some more goats and cows so that father could afford to return the original without loss. And as for the bottles of London Dry Gin I could finance those myself. Then my clothes and jewellery too were left untouched and I had brought them along. But father had used the goats and cows to remarry, and he definitely was not going to agree to my wish. So instead I said after all the rebukes that I had just come to the village to have my child. And this message too I sent to Akobi in the city.

5

My child Kofo sought his way out of my belly into the world one Friday dawn nearly seven weeks after I arrived in the village, a tough, bouncing, big-eyed baby boy. I was proud. He was outdoored on the seventh day and for the first time since I left the city Akobi came to the village. He had to be there for his first son's outdooring.

The very next day he announced he was leaving for the city because work was awaiting him. To my surprise, he insisted on taking with him the high-quality gold jewellery that his father had presented to me in gratitude for his first grandson, as well as the cloth and other jewellery given me as dowry, which I brought with me from the city. When I asked to know why he told me simply, 'For safekeeping.'

I had no reason not to believe him. But barely hours after his departure from the village I began having doubtful fears when rumours reached us that Akobi had left so soon not because work awaited him but because he had had a nasty row with his father. His father had flatly refused to give in to his demand that he should sell part of his farmlands and give him the money for some project he was about to undertake which would, guaranteed, bring in plenty of money. Now, I thought, just a moment; if he didn't get the money from his father then that must be why he has taken off with my cloth and gold jewellery. Already there was the money he once borrowed from his father which he had saved. And a large part of his salary too he always saved since apart from the rent he paid nothing more, our daily meals having become my sole responsibility. And he had hinted too, more than once, that he was saving his money for more important things. My thought now was: what was Akobi's important project?

I heard nothing more from Akobi for about ten more months during which I continued living in the village, helping on the farm and selling palmwine at weekends. Akobi's father was generous and took good care of his grandson. When Kofo was nearing a year I began to plan my return to the city to trade properly. My only problem was how the three of us would cope in our two-by-four room. But that problem my mother solved when she woke me up in the night and said there was something she urgently needed to talk to me about. Akobi's father was not pleased that I was returning with his only grandson to the city and had clandestinely approached her to solicit her help in convincing me to leave my son behind in the village and return to the city alone. Mother, who had thought that I would raise hell in protest, was completely taken aback when, ignoring her anxious plea that I take time to think about it, I immediately replied, 'Good. I will leave him here.' So, a year after my separation from Akobi, I left Kofo with my mother and, carrying as much as my wicker basket would hold, headed back to the city one Saturday morning and back to this man Akobi who was still my husband. A staggering surprise awaited me.

Anxious to lay eyes once more on my gold jewellery which in the true sense of the word was my only life insurance, the only property I owned in life, I looked for it in the place where I knew Akobi was likely to keep it. I looked and searched and found nothing; neither the jewellery nor my new clothes. And the costly waist-beads I inherited from my grandmother when she died I didn't find. Plus other little things, all of which were gone, even the little delicate ebony carving mother had given me the first time I was leaving for the city as my protector. The tearful doubts I had already had back in the village returned. I prayed desperately that for once my instincts would be proved wrong.

Suppressing the hysteria building up in me and threatening to explode, I headed to Mama Kiosk to tell her I was back and to thank her for the baby things and talcum powder she had sent to me in the village. I approached her door, knocked, and heard her

31

footsteps approach. She swung her door wide open, stood in its space, her face lighting up with a broad smile; then she laughed exuberantly, cupped me in her arms, led me into the room and gave me water to drink, returned and sat down facing me and set her eyes upon my face searchingly. I saw at once she had something heavy on her chest. 'Is something wrong, Mama Kiosk?' I asked suspiciously. All I got from her was, 'You are a good woman, Greenhorn, a very good young woman.'

'Not as good as you intone, Mama Kiosk,' I said, 'but won't you tell me what is wrong?'

She didn't. All she added was, 'Mara, if I haven't heard news from the horse's own mouth I don't carry it further. Ask your husband.'

So thirty minutes later I left her place an even more confused woman, to return to mine.

Akobi returned home after midnight. I hadn't informed him beforehand that I was coming. To minimise the surprise I knew my presence would cause him, I laid out my mat on the floor and slept on it. He didn't disturb me. Indeed, next morning it was as if I hadn't been away for a year and just returned. A resumption of the same daily routine followed: up at dawn to warm water, carry his things for him to the bathhouse, wait for him to wash, carry bucket and bath accessories back, clean the house and cook the food and then go throw people's rubbish away for them for foodstuffs.

'Oh Mara you are back! How beautiful!' all exclaimed. And nothing hurt more than knowing that it wasn't beautiful that I was back but that I was back to resume throwing their filth away for them; me with my nose that had nothing against inhaling the stench of the rubbish dump and the public toilet by it, if even for just two fingers of plantain. Me, greenhorn Mara, their nose saviour, was back in full swing.

Then came the awaited shock.

'Akobi,' I said on the Sunday morning, 'yesterday I searched for my jewellery and clothes and other things but I didn't find them. Did you put them here?'

He was lying face up on the mattress.

'No,' he replied curtly.

'You said you were bringing them for safekeeping but I didn't find them here,' I went on desperately.

'Because they are not here,' he replied off-handedly, his face searching the corrugated-sheet ceiling.

'Where are they?' I said at last.

'I've sold them!' he replied, still looking at the ceiling.

'You what!!!' I said, making a grab at the armchair for support.

'I sold them. And now go and see to my porridge,' he ordered.

I didn't know if that was meant as a threat or just what it was, an order. But I wasn't afraid. I stood my ground.

'Can you tell me why you sold them?' I screamed. 'What did you do with the money? Did you buy a bus? Some land? Or maybe a house?'

But he remained surprisingly calm. 'No,' he replied, 'I deposited the money for my passport and a ticket. I am travelling to Europe!'

I wanted to scream but all that came out was a whine. Oh dear, I thought to myself, I left my husband for too long alone in the city and now he is going mad.

'Please answer me truly, Akobi,' I pleaded.

'Didn't you hear? Go and see to my porridge!'

'No!! I didn't hear, Akobi,' I screamed back so stubbornly and defiantly that I could read shock on his face.

'You are not going to do what I said?' he shot back threateningly. But this time I was prepared for it. I was prepared for him and for everything, anything that came up and I didn't care which form it took.

He sat up on the mattress and straightaway I snatched one of the piled broken block pieces supporting the fourth leg of the centre table, bringing the table down.

'No Akobi,' I hissed threateningly, 'this time I am not going to do what you say. You are going to tell me what you did with my property.' And I aimed the concrete piece directly at him. For the first ever time in my whole married life I saw that Akobi was unsure. He was unsure whether to take my threat to hit him with the concrete piece seriously or as a bluff. I was that angry because I didn't, couldn't believe all this about Europe. My God, how could I? Europe to me was a place so special and so very,

very far away, somewhere unimaginable, maybe even somewhere near Heaven, where not just anybody could go. A place where only the very rich, those Ministers, the big doctors and lawyers who learned plenty of books and married white women could go. But Akobi? My own husband Akobi with this his two-by-four corrugated-iron-sheet home situated by a public toilet and rubbish dump? This my Akobi whose father's wealth depended on how often cholera or dysentry struck Naka and its surrounding villages? No! I was certain he had gone and given my jewellery to some woman, maybe that Ministries woman, Comfort. That was why I raged. As for Europe, it was out. How could it be true? It just couldn't. But it was. And it was me who was wrong. Akobi knew more than I did. He had more confidence in himself than I had ever imagined, and seemed to know exactly what he was after. After he had successfully cooled me down by telling me to forget the porridge and to please allow him to explain it all to me, he proceeded to convince me of his plan.

'I am going to Europe to live there for just a year or two at most,' he began, 'and to work. Mara, do you know that there is so plenty factory and construction work waiting to be done there in Europe but with so little people to do them? That is why I sold your things, Mara. I want to go there and work, to work hard. And I tell you, I tell you upon the gods of Naka that, Mara, in a year, in just one year, you will see for yourself. I will make so much money that I can buy us everything! Everything, Mara! Television, radio, fridge, carpet, even car!'

'Car!!' I exclaimed, flabbergasted, unconsciously dropping the piece of brick I had been holding all the while. 'Car, you said?'

'And that won't be all, Mara,' he went on, 'that would be just the first year. If I don't miss you and Kofo too much by then' (as though he had missed us the whole year I'd been in Naka) 'and I am able to stay on for another year or more, then before I return we can have our own home. A beautiful block house just like those government Ministers and doctors with their English wives have. All that Mara, all that! Can you imagine?'

Stupid question. Of course I couldn't imagine. How could I? Ah, when we were young in Naka we used to imagine Europe not to be just near Heaven but in Heaven itself: 'That is why

34

people who go there return very beautiful,' said one. And another supported it with, 'And that must be why only these flying things can go there!'

I didn't know then what aeroplanes were. And even though I now knew, from my stay in the city, Europe was still for me something far away. But now I let the thought sink gradually deep into me till I began trembling and my heart began to pound unnaturally fast with excitement. So carried away was I at that moment that if Akobi had suggested there and then a wish to sell me, in addition to my clothes and jewellery, I would gladly have agreed.

'Akobi, you are sure all this is indeed possible?' I asked eventually, desperately seeking reassurance, frantically wanting to hear more of it. And I got it. Akobi grinned pompously as I had often seen our giant-nosed Naka chief grin in his palanquin and replied, 'Possible? Ah, Mara, would I lie to you? More than possible. Far, far more than possible, I tell you. Ho, do you know for instance that in Britain the people are so rich that they throw fridges away? And in Germany they throw cars away?'

'They what?' I howled like a wolf. I simply had to. 'They throw fridges and cars away?'

'That is what I am saying, Mara,' replied Akobi, still wearing his pompous grin.

'And they are correct in their heads? The white people in Europe?' I asked seriously for I was more than convinced that people who threw fridges and cars away couldn't be right in their heads, but Akobi had a ready answer for here too.

'Correct in their heads? Hm,' he chuckled, 'they are more than correct in their heads, Mara. Very correct. What do you think? They throw these things away because they simply have too much. That is all.'

But that was still too much for me. I just could not let myself believe that a person who was correct in the head would throw away fridges and cars. Ah, here if you had no such gadgets you were a nothing. You could have a television that was spoilt. It didn't matter. You probably did not even watch it or, if you did, you didn't understand anything on it for why should you if it was all full of Simon Templar running up and down boxing people unconscious, shooting them dead and kissing long-legged blonds when you yourself had not seen a gun before, knew nothing of something called Scotland Yard and had never seen your parents kiss? But that didn't matter. What mattered was that you had a television. And if as well as the television you had a fridge and a car, then, eh, between you and the Minister or doctor only his English wife separated you. Where he stepped or spat, you too could step or spit. And such a prestige it was that Akobi was aiming at? It was too sweet to be true, simply too sweet to be believed without fear. But not for my dear Akobi. He went on cool-headedly, mesmerising, enticing, luring.

'Mara,' he called suddenly, adjusting himself pompously, 'tell me, what business do you think is better? A corn-grinding machine or a dough-mixer? Or maybe a rice harvester? We can hire it out to farmers in the north for big sums of money and large bags of rice. What do you think?'

What did I think? I choked. My God, it was the first time he was asking my opinion on anything . . .

'Akobi,' I said dreamily, 'whatever you say I am sure is the right thing. What you decide on I am sure is the right thing. I am sure Akobi.' And it was like I was in the middle of a dream, being made love to by Don Juan. There was nothing Akobi would have said at that moment that I wouldn't have done. His word at that moment was holy. And not even the Pope could have thwarted me. If Akobi had suddenly suggested that I allowed myself to be beheaded, that cutting my head off at that moment was the right thing to do, I would readily and gladly have given in and still gone hopping headless, singing hallelujah unto him. So taken in was I by him. And that was even before I heard what he had in store for me personally.

'Mara,' he began, 'please don't think that I am ashamed of you or anything like that, you hear, but please, while I am away I want you too to learn sewing because when I am coming back from Europe I will bring you six or eight electric sewing machines so that you can open your own sewing salon here in the city. Do you think that you can learn to sew in two years?'

I didn't reply. I couldn't. The sheer pleasure of hearing this, of existing in the room at that moment and of having Akobi as my husband and father of my son filled me with such intense pleasure that it threatened to explode. I was swaying with sweet drunkenness. I moved towards him on the mattress, 'Akobi,' I called his name feebly, 'I must lie down a bit. I fear if I don't I might faint.' And I meant it.

He smiled a little wry smile and stretched himself out beside me on the mattress too. He yawned, sighed and closed his eyes, the wry smile still on his face. He had won. And he knew it.

6

I was a woman walking on air and the lightness in my head was like it was resting peacefully on the giant bosom of a Goddess unknown. When I walked on the street and cars passed me by I just smiled my knowing smile for I knew that it was only a matter of time and someone else would be walking that street while I passed by in a car. When I was very thirsty and I treated myself to the rare luxury of an ice-cooled bottle of water from a kiosk instead of a calabash of tap water I smiled my knowing smile for I knew that only time and I would be drinking from my own fridge. Ah, it was a very good feeling but not without its price. Akobi told me that even though he had now raised enough for the most important expenses there were still a couple little expenses more to be met and he had to save every penny for it. In other words, I was to tighten my belt even more. So, filled with all the hopes this world could offer, I put everything into work to earn more and more. I couldn't hawk at the lorry station because Mama Kiosk had brought me the message that Esiama and her pot-bellied lover were demanding that I came there to kneel before her and apologise in the presence of all who were there when I fought her before I could resume hawking. And since I wasn't prepared to subject myself to such belittlement, especially at a time when my husband was soon to become a 'been-to', I sent back a message to Esiama that if she was waiting for me to come and apologise to her then she would have a long wait and could put her time to better use by resuming the search for her missing teeth in the sand. Then I sought an alternative place where I could hawk, and settled on the train station. But it was a place where a lot of women already hawked boiled eggs so I cut down my eggs by a third and also hawked roasted groundnuts to go with banana. It was a wise decision because I made excellent business with it. Then I also took up selling cheap tobacco at the night market, and, when time permitted on Sundays, fresh coconuts at the beach. All this I did wholeheartedly because suddenly no work was too hard or too strenuous for me so long as it would go to seeing Akobi realise his plans. So that soon not only was I the sole provider of our daily meals but the sole payer of our rent too because every penny that Akobi made became his and his alone. Then his travel plans neared their final stages, which included the people of our village hearing of them and the excitement that gripped Naka as a result was indescribable. 'This is the big God's sign to show the world that Naka is his chosen land,' proclaimed someone.

'And the people of Naka, his chosen people,' supported another.

'Akobi has brought a great honour to this village,' announced the chief, and made known his intention to bestow honour on Akobi's family in reciprocation by taking on one of his sisters for his seventeenth wife. So all of Naka became involved in Akobi's travel plans. Every day, people stood and waited anxiously for news of how far his preparations had gone. But as mother would say, it was the over-confidence of the hare that made the tortoise beat him in the race.

Akobi had got his passport after heavily bribing someone at the passport office. He had deposited money for his ticket and even bought a brand new portmanteau, a couple of new shirts, trousers, ties and shoes. But still he had no entry visa for any European country. Then came a man somewhere along the line who claimed to have connections at embassies and said he could push through Akobi's visa. He took a large sum of money which he said he would need to bribe his connections; then he disappeared, just as he had materialised, without a trace.

I don't know who else apart from me Akobi told this problem to and whether he deliberately intended it to reach the ears of the people of Naka but, whatever it was, there was one group that must have cursed him for having hinted at the problem to anyone, namely the hens and goats of Naka. For, no sooner had rumours of the problem reached the village than the hens and goats saw their funerals come quicker than they ever anticipated as one villager after another went offering sacrifices to the medicine man on behalf of Akobi in order, as they put it, to enable him to wrench the problem at its neck.

Maybe the gods were not too pleased about the hens and goats, I don't know. Or maybe they were angry that the villagers brought local gin instead of the better-quality London Dry Gin which the medicine man (who drinks it on the gods' behalf) claims the gods prefer, I can't say. But Akobi did not succeed in wrenching the problem at its neck, and ending up with a visa. All that happened was that he borrowed and manoeuvred and finally learnt there was a way – an expensive way – of entering Europe without a visa. But the sum of money demanded was one that Akobi couldn't raise for at least another year, even if he saved every penny of his monthly salary. That was how it came about that his father, who had meanwhile regretted his refusal of Akobi's earlier request for money, seeing the even greater prestige his son's travel ambition had brought him, now approached Akobi to please allow him to provide the needed money. This he had raised by selling the plot of land he had initially refused to sell, and by his sister, Akobi's aunt, selling some of her gold jewellery. And upon a brightly woven cloth laid out on a small wooden plate he presented the money to Akobi. So now there was no stopping Akobi. The way was his front, as Mama Kiosk would say. And everyone shared in his excitement.

Gradually his day of departure approached. And then it was just two days away and his office co-workers pulled resources together and organised a farewell party for him at the Lido Club. I didn't attend the party. Akobi insisted he must go alone because his colleagues would definitely recognise me as the woman who used to stand by him at the bus stop in faded clothes and tyre slippers. And this would be catastrophic for him. As I did not want to cause him any catastrophe, with his departure just two days away, I gave in without a murmur, especially because he sweetly promised to be back by all means around midnight. And I believed him. But he didn't come at midnight. Indeed he came the following day at ten o'clock in the morning only to leave again without a word of explanation. Then he didn't return until eight at night, by which time through Mama Kiosk – who knew virtually all the regulars that visited the Lido Club, and the workers too – the gossip had reached my ears that indeed it was a great show-off farewell party, naturally with Akobi as the centre man, but also that while I sat at home he had proudly announced to the giddily excited crowd that this woman, Comfort, who had once given him the cold shoulder, was his woman for life. And as if to confirm it, he left ostentatiously with her to go to her place. So there it was he spent the night and probably too the next day. Yet, although it worried me, I raised no objection for after all polygamy was inherent in my upbringing and tolerance was the code word here. Just so long as I didn't witness or hear him sleep with the other woman! But it left a fear in me as, on further reflection, I started seeing him returning from Europe, a been-to, seeing this woman Comfort as the more appropriate woman to be at his side, and him discarding me in spite of all my sweat and labour. I knew this was something Comfort wouldn't turn down even for promises of five bungalows and ten Morris Minors, for after all she had been snubbing Akobi all this while, so her sudden change of mind must be for one reason only – that Akobi was travelling to Europe. And a young been-to husband was certainly more to be appreciated than a flabby-bellied married top man who didn't keep his promises of bungalows and Morris Minors.

When he returned that evening he said he wouldn't eat. He had eaten already, he added, and went straight to bed. I had barely lowered the kerosene lamp when there was a loud continuous banging on our door with the all too familiar voice of Mama Kiosk shouting my name and asking me to wake up my husband and to come immediately with him. Akobi was initially reluctant to get out of bed, intending to ignore the calls. But the persistence of Mama Kiosk and her frantic calls that it had to do with his journey, which not to forget was the very next day, got him jumping out of bed and rushing out of the door, with me after him. Who should confront us out there but an assistant of

41

the medicine man back in the village, come all the way from Naka to offer a last-minute warning from his master. He was covered in dust and said it was because he had walked all the way from the lorry station; and had also had plenty problems finding our place. He accepted the calabash full of water that I offered him, took in a mouthful of it, after having poured libation to the gods under the earth, and said he had just come to give a message from his lord and master the medicine man and to return immediately: something I must say did not displease me at all since already my head was aching with the question of where he would sleep.

The message was brisk, urgent and precise: 'Shake hands with no one at the airport tomorrow. Someone is intending to plant bad medicine at the last minute inside your palm so that all will go wrong for you in Europe!' That was it. And true to his word, he turned and left.

It may sound funny, the message, maybe even silly, too, that for these two sentences a man must be made to journey all the way from the village to the city, a distance of very many kilometres; but not for superstitious people like us. And definitely not when it had to do with a subject like a trip to Europe. So until deep into the night we banged our heads together with Mama Kiosk to find a way whereby this handshake would be avoided without raising suspicions of a superstition in play, for, oh hell! that wouldn't pass at all in the 'noble' picture of Akobi in his grey suit, striped tie and pointed shoes, waiting to board a plane to Europe. That was the conflict of our complexes, you see. A superstitious African man travelling to the continent of civilis-ation will do everything to hide from everybody that he is superstitious (even though everybody knows that he is) because superstition is regarded as primitive. And the about-to-become 'been-to' is naturally the last person who will want to be connected with primitiveness. But we cracked and cracked our heads and failed to come up with any solution for, after all, the handshakes at the airport were an unavoidable and integral part of the whole ritual of journeying to Europe. A departure at the airport without a handshake? That was as unimaginable as it was suspicious. And yet, there was the medicine man's warning.

42

By the morning we still had not found a solution. But there still was a bit more time since his take-off time was 11 p.m. and the man whom he had paid to smuggle him to Europe (since he had no entry visa), an underground agent of some sort, was not due to come for him till between 7 p.m. and 8 p.m.

I knew without being told that if I wasn't welcome at the farewell party two days ago then I wasn't welcome at the airport either. But I comforted my soul with the thought that till 7 p.m. at least, I had him still. An error!

At 2 p.m. I left the room to go to buy charcoal for the fire, so that I could prepare his favourite crab soup for him as my farewell gift. On my return barely twenty minutes later, Akobi had gone without a trace. One neighbour said that as soon as I had left she had seen him leave with his portmanteau, the very one he was travelling with, but all by himself and in the same casual wear he had put on when he got up. So I thought he'd probably just gone to have some last-minute thing done to his portmanteau, that maybe it was even to do with a plan he'd suddenly come up with for dealing with the handshake problem. Besides, he had left no message for me. Even though in the past he never left messages for me when he was going out in my absence, I felt that since this involved a journey, he definitely would make an exception of it. So I went ahead and prepared the soup, made it all ready for him and settled down and patiently waited for his return. I sat and sat and waited and waited. The seconds ticked into minutes and the minutes into hours and still I sat and waited and hoped . . . till 7 p.m. came, and I knew I had sat and waited and hoped in vain. My big bowl of soup sat there, the yams I had peeled ready to cook sat there, the bowl of water placed ready for him to wash his hands before and after eating sat there, and I also sat there, my hopes crumbled, trampled and shattered.

The rest of the time went much more quickly. And when the clock ticked 11 p.m., the time I knew his plane would be taking off, I rose slowly, picked up the bowl of soup, walked to the farthest end of the stinking gutter and emptied the entire contents of the bowl into it. I did the same too with the water, and the yams too found their way into the rubbish bin. When I had

43

finished I walked back into our room, took his old towel, hopped into the grass bed, clutched the towel intimately to myself and cried my whole God-given eyeballs out. I was an irony unto my own self. This towel I clutched intimately to myself had many a time caused me beatings, like when it stubbornly refused to dry up because the weather was damp during the night and in its wet state I offered it to Akobi in the morning. I got beaten as though it was me in control of the world's weather. As though I caused the dampness. And yet here I was clutching it to myself like a child would her favourite teddy bear. And why at all was I crying? What precious wonder at all was Akobi to me that I should cry because he was gone? Didn't he make more a maid out of me than a wife? And yet here was I crying because he was gone; because no longer would I receive his beatings, his kicks, his slaps, scolds and humiliations. And through it all I saw one thing clearly – unknowingly and unconsciously to my own self, I had grown wholly attached to Akobi, to his unfairness, to his bullying, to the strength he possessed over me. I didn't like what he meted out to me with that strength and yet, at the same time, that same strength made me acknowledge him as the man of the house; as my husband. Or maybe too I was afraid of change, of the unknown, this new situation where I was now to be my own master. What was it going to be like living without Akobi's dominance, the very dominance I so feared and loathed? Was I capable of being a master even unto my own self? I just was so used to being the servant. Ah, spirits of the land, I so feared this change; and this fear it was (I think) that made me want Akobi back, that made me wish and desire his presence. And that probably was why I cried so.

7

Akobi had been gone two weeks and I was sitting and talking to Mama Kiosk when she said suddenly, 'Greenhorn, there is something I have been wanting to tell you for some time now . . .'

'What?' I shot in suspiciously.

'Your husband, Greenhorn.'

'His hand?' I was thinking about the controversy over the handshake.

'No no . . . oh that! I hear he had his hands full and gave that as excuse why he couldn't shake hands. But no, Greenhorn. That's not what I am talking about. It's this his other woman, Comfort. She was the reason why he left you early and without even a proper good-bye. It was to be with her.'

It was somehow funny that Mama Kiosk should be telling me things that I, as Akobi's wife, should have known and be telling Mama Kiosk, like for instance, this thing that he did with his hands. But regarding the business with Comfort, it wasn't strange that I didn't know. Cheated wives are almost always the last people to know what is being done to them by the husbands. Still, that twinge of fear returned, that suspicion and uncertainty that I wouldn't be good enough for Akobi when he returned. I whimpered, my face all hot with this fear eating me: 'He went there again?'

'Yes,' Mama Kiosk replied, 'and not just that, Greenhorn. It was her who saw him off at the airport. To tell you the truth, Greenhorn, if I was you, now that he's gone I would forget him and start thinking wholly about yourself and your son. That is what you must do. These our men they always leave for Europe and say they'll be back in one two or three years. "I am only going there to work and make money and return" is what they all say, but they go and they never return again. You must forget him!'

I was horrified, to say the least. What was this that Mama Kiosk was telling me? Forget Akobi?

'I have plenty respect for you Mama Kiosk,' I began calculatingly, my bile rising into my throat at what I considered Mama Kiosk going overboard, 'and I look up to you many times as my mother. And you are so good to me too. But I don't like this that you are saying to me, Mama Kiosk. I don't like it at all.'

'Good,' said Mama Kiosk eventually with a surprising calmness, 'then do what you think is best for you, Mara. But don't ever say your Mama Kiosk didn't warn you.'

And I knew that she was dead serious about it because she calls me Mara only when she is dead serious about something.

Alone in bed that night I decided that I would begin taking the steps to do something about myself that would make Akobi proud of me when he returned, that would remove all doubts that I was as good as his Comfort. I thought hard. First, I would continue hawking my eggs and groundnuts to enable me to finance my sewing lessons. And then when I had qualified as a seamstress I would seek an apprentice job with an established seamstress and start taking full care of myself – cosmetics, my hair, dresses and shoes. I would transform myself so much that even Akobi wouldn't be able to recognise me on return until I told him: Behold! here is your Mara who stands before you!! And then we'll see about those glittering no-good women at the Ministries. And upon this decision, I swore a solemn oath.

Six weeks later I went to the government hospital to complain that I was feeling funny. The symptoms were not unknown to me, but I had had my period normally the previous month and had no reason therefore to think that I was pregnant again. But I was. And even though there was no Akobi around this time to beat me for it, I still was not certain I could cope with it alone. Suspending all my sworn plans, I left as early as the fourth month of my pregnancy and went back to live with my mother and son in the village. That was when I realised that the city had gotten under my skin. Each passing day, awaiting the arrival of my second child, was like a year to me, because I was no longer able to identify with and integrate back into village life. I had sampled city life. I had staunchly planted inside my head the idea of becoming a seamstress and transforming myself into a modern woman for Akobi. I had set myself an end that would make me more acceptable to my been-to husband, and it was all that my daily thoughts revolved around. Naturally I had to help on the farm to make up for my upkeep and shelter. And I had to sell palmwine too to make money for Alhaji's monthly rent back in the city. But all this I did only half-heartedly, for so it was when one lived long enough in the city and got infected with this that I call 'city disease'. City life was so drastically different from village life that once one allowed oneself to get infected, reverting to village life was like cycling uphill. When one had plans as I did, then the will even to try to revert to the relatively more organised village life was non-existent. So when the time came for me to return to the city after my second son had turned eight months, I was a bundle of joy itself. And in spite of my little rebellion just before I had left, I arrived back into the readily warm waiting arms of Mama Kiosk.

There was no time to waste. I set frantically about fulfilling my ambition and the first thing I did was seek a seamstress who would teach me to sew. As to earning money, I abandoned hawking eggs and took to frying pancakes for sale at the marketplace in the afternoons because mornings I attended my sewing lessons, while nights and weekends saw me selling sweets and cigarettes in front of the cinema houses. My change of trade was for the simple reason that I considered it to be more civilised than hawking eggs and groundnuts. In short, more compatible with the new me I had set out to be.

As for the fact that Akobi was in Europe, the more days and months that passed, the more the thought of it elated me. When I thought, too, that one day soon I would own my own sewing home, as Akobi had made clear he intended for me, I simply floated above clouds. Many times in my daydreams I vividly imagined what it would look like, this my sewing home in

47

prospect, and how I would call it Mara's Modern Sewing Corner, or Mara's Psychedelic Sewing Home, for psychedelic was one of the new hip words around, and these were part of the ever-popular city life. New words come and go and people coin different meanings for them in addition to what the dictionary says they mean, just so that they can be used more often. Once, it was 'afro buddy'. While several barber shops promptly re-named their businesses Afro Buddy Corner, Afro Buddy Hair Styles, Your Own Sharp Afro Buddy Trim Base, and what have you, an obscure shoe repairer too sprang up from nowhere and fiercely started the rumours that Afro Buddy was also a style of walking in Harlem, a style that could be walked with only a particular kind of shoe sole that automatically tilts the walker to the right because the sole of his right shoe is sawn off shorter toward the outside, leaving an intact sole for the left shoe and a deformed slanted sole for the right. Believe it or not, shoe repairers (rather ironic since in this case they were anything but repairing shoes) north, south, east and west began doing brisk overtime sawing off the right soles of people's shoes, old and new, large and small, black and brown. All arrived in their plenty at the repairers' kiosks and left deformed. And all men in the city were doing the afro buddy walk, just because someone said it was the walk being walked in Harlem. Harlem, Brixton, Brook-lyn – they were the magic names in the city. And whatever was claimed to have come from there, became the 'in' thing.

I needed plenty changes outside me still, I knew, but I had started and made significant strides and was content with my steady progress. For instance, I no longer wore African cloth, neither new nor old. No! I wore dresses, European dresses. Madam Anaba, my seamstress teacher, helped me make them. You know, it sounds nothing special, said just simply: I no longer wore cloth, I wore dresses. But it was something special. It was an outward transformation and it was a thrill, a very special and subjective thrill. It was like a young woman from a very strict Moslem country who for years and years had worn nothing else but this long black Tschador and suddenly one day, there she is, in a casual summer mini-dress, reaching way up above her knees, God's free air blowing alluringly between her thighs and around and over her legs. She looks at herself in the mirror and she asks herself, Why didn't I do this before? That was what I asked myself too: Why didn't I start wearing dresses when Akobi was here? It was such a transformation and I would have passed better into his world, his modern world. It probably would have made him take me to his farewell party and to the airport and there probably would never have been the need for Comfort's intrusion into his life. But that too was in the past now. The present and the future were what mattered and I was changing quite fast for it; the change that would make Akobi not hesitate to show me off to his friends; the change that he wished of his wife, wanted of me, but never trusted me to achieve.

I kept my sworn promise to myself and progressed fast with my sewing. But with nearly two years since his departure, all that we had heard from Akobi was one postcard and a brief letter that said he was still settling and would write again as soon as he had settled. This settling, it seemed, was taking far longer than any of us anticipated. Two years it was he said he would need to work and make the money of his dreams. And the end of the two years was fast approaching and still there was no trace at all of any of the televisions and cars, the grinding machine and the rice harvester, not forgetting – most importantly of course – my six electric sewing machines. So what now? Many a time I felt Mama Kiosk's eyes burrow deep into my face as if to say: Well, I told you so, didn't I? But she had the good sense never to let it leave her lips.

The frail old professional letter-writer always seated behind his old cracky typewriter in front of the post office became my friend, because virtually every week I went to him to write a letter to Akobi. I had just so many requests and suggestions to make to him, especially regarding my sewing machines, that I even made the fact that he had not replied to even one of my many letters deliberately escape me. I needed a machine that sewed zig-zag on all sizes, so I wrote and told him. I needed a beautiful bodice and corset that would hold my flabby rump in order – something that became vividly clear to me when I ceased wearing cloth and started wearing dresses – so that, too, I wrote

49

and told him. I found out that machine bobbins were very expensive on the home market but were available for plenty a pound in Europe. So that, too, I wrote and told him. Then of course there was the thread . . .

> Dear my one and only Akobi, (was how the old letter writer began)
> I forgot to tell you about thread in my last letter. Please don't forget, when you are coming, to buy and bring with you large bundles of thread of all colours, especially red, because red is now the psychedelic colour that people wear. Even I, too, I have sewn one red dress.
> Bye-bye,
> Your wife Mara of the City.

I always felt that it was extremely important that I added the 'of the city', just in case some friend of his should read it and think I was still a village woman. So, on and on I wrote to Akobi, and on and on went the silence: no replies. Then one day something happened: my letter was returned to me. I re-posted it, having re-checked the stamps, on Mama Kiosk's advice. But yet again I got it back. From then on whatever letter I wrote, I got it promptly back with a large RETURN TO SENDER in red capitals on the envelope. I began to worry, and Akobi's father and family too began to worry. Two years had gone and the expected car that would roll the narrow roads of Naka had still not materialised. His father was beginning to hate himself for having given in at long last and sold his farmland, and his aunt was already fighting with his father for having talked her into making her sell her gold ornaments for him. The chief, too, was suddenly unsure that he truly wanted Akobi's sister as his last wife (it was a special honour to be the last wife since it invariably meant that you gave the man all he wanted so that he didn't see the usefulness of taking on a new wife) and was already planning on two more wives. And my father's brief glory as the father-in-law of Akobi began to dwindle fast. Things were getting rough and everyone was blaming everyone else but himself for everything, from why Akobi was sent to school in the first place to why this his trip to Europe received encouragement.

Just when everyone was about to throw in the towel and concede that it had all been just a gamble that had not paid off, Akobi wrote.

The letter was long and full and in it he said that he had changed his address which was why we didn't hear from him for so long; also, he had so much to sort out. Well, first he was settling and now he was sorting things out. Skepticism was already brewing, when on the second sheet a bombshell dropped that shattered all doubts and anger: Akobi wanted ME to join him in Europe!!

> . . . I have saved plenty money for all the things I am
> intending to buy (he wrote on) but I want to save a bit more
> because of the shipment costs, and at a faster rate than before.
> But the factory jobs here, they are so hard and so strenuous
> that I can do two jobs a day or plenty overtime, which is what
> I am planning, only if Mara can be here to keep house for me.
> I am entreating your help for it. Someone is visiting home. He
> is an Agent and I know him well. He will be spending just a
> few weeks at home. When he returns I want him to come with
> Mara. I have taken care of everything this end, the contract
> cost and the ticket. You only need to do a handful of things
> for Mara, like her passport and the few things she will need
> for the journey. You must keep your heads high because this
> your son of Naka is on to great things and will not let you
> down. And upon the scalps of the gods I sign off here in
> peace.
>
> Your own Akobi.

The letter was translated into our language and its contents repeated to all the village. Before long, all Naka was back in Akobi fever again, and two young women who not long ago were swimming in seventh heaven were now in tears of sorrow because the chief was suddenly no longer sure that he did indeed want them that much to take them on as his wives. My mother, who had never been able to afford a portmanteau for herself, promised to sell some of her inherited beads to get me one, after I told her that I could just about afford only the required bribes for my passport. Akobi's family said they would take care of our two sons. I stopped attending my sewing lessons so that I could save what otherwise would be my fees, since, as Madam Anaba put it, 'You can learn more psychedelic sewing in Europe,' and for my farewell gift, she gave me two red dresses. Mama Kiosk, too, stood ground on my behalf and vigorously fought with Alhaji about some repair work he said he'd have to carry out on my roof, just so that I could save that money too. Alhaji, angered and shocked at this daring challenge to his authority, said he wanted me out of his 'house' by the following week. Then he returned very mellowed and very 'un-Alhaji-like' in the evening and said I shouldn't take seriously his threat of earlier on. Lest you think that Alhaji had seen some holy light and repented . . . NO! He hadn't. He had just learned that my husband was in Europe and I was going soon to join him there. And what better reason was there to campaign for yet another increase in rent than that? Even two of his former tenants had now travelled to Europe, he said. Forget the fact that this makes it sound as though living in his corrugated-iron-sheet shelter automatically made us land in Europe. Alhaji was not one to scrutinise things that way. So my daily trips to the passport office began and it became necessary for me to approach mother and beg her to sell yet more of her beads because one clerk there wanted to sleep with me before he pushed through my passport form, even before it got to the stage where I knew I would have to pay the bribes. This hitch I hadn't calculated and reckoned with, so I blew my top and queried the clerk, whose face was like unevenly kneaded dough, if he knew who he was talking to that way. 'My husband is in Europe, you hear! And I myself am going to join him soon, you hear! So don't talk to me like that at all, you hear!'

The dough-faced clerk waited very patiently till I was thoroughly through with my outburst and said very coolly, 'You want your form to leave my desk, pay!' And shoved it under a high pile of other forms.

So that was it! If I felt too big in my shoes to sleep with him because my husband was living in Europe and I myself was soon to go and join him, then I must do what people in big shoes, like I was shoving myself into, do: PAY! And pay I did. In the end, when I calculated, the bribes I had paid could have fed my whole family in the village for maybe a year or so. But I got my passport, which was what I wanted. And my preparations to go and join Akobi feverishly began.

8

That I was travelling to Europe raised me in the esteem of my family in the village so much that mother didn't even care any longer about the beads she had to sell. Suddenly, people were greeting her with low respectful bows and mothers were warning their children to handle my two sons with respect and care during play. From the city, too, Esiama sent a message to me through Mama Kiosk that she had forgotten our fight and that she and her driver lover even wanted to shake hands with me if time would allow me to come over to the station before I left for Europe. True to their word, when I went strolling there one afternoon just out of curiosity, since I knew that all there knew about my impending travel, Esiama came and greeted me and her lover even offered me a bottle of cool beer which I equally coolly refused with the excuse that it was too bitter, though the truth was that I didn't want to drink his beer just in case he one day should use it to blackmail my conscience. But one thing, though, was that I learnt fast and quick. So dramatically could things change; so magically could Europe work on attitudes. I was living it at the receiving end and enjoying every minute of it. Just as it affected people's attitudes, so too did it affect my confidence; so much so that I was even able to go for a stroll around the compounds of the Ministries – something I never before then would have dared to do – clad in a red dress and summer sandals, my hair not plaited but afro-combed. Ah! ah Mpoipoi, you goddess of beauty, I sure could even have been able to look this Comfort girl right in the eye and scrutinise the

54

size of her pupils if she had materialised before me. She was probably seated there somewhere in one of those many offices behind some dingy typewriter and thinking of her last days with Akobi my husband, I thought to myself with satisfaction and smiled a wry smile. The day of judgement had come and now we were seeing who was the wife. I thought on. If only I could see her before I left so I could say it to her face. Yes, I was that confident and I walked tall, head high. I radiated self-confidence and it didn't awe me at all when some of the pretty Ministries women even greeted me with their green violet and blue painted eyelids and scarlet smeared lips. I, illiterate Mara, had turned into a modern woman, body and soul; a caricature pseudo-Euro-transformation that brought with it its caricature pseudo-high feel. I felt a new me.

Much against my will, however (since I considered it incompatible with this new 'modern' and 'civilised' me), I visited the village medicine man a few days before my departure on the insistence of my mother who said (and I agreed with her) that it was better than suddenly being told at the last minute that I shouldn't, say, shake hands with anyone at the airport, or who knows what would have come up in my case. So I went. And what a ritual! The medicine man (naturally, after I had met his demand of a bottle of London Dry Gin and a pure white fat hen) covered me from head to toe with white powder, mixed a pounded mixture of herbs and the dried marrow of some unnamed wild animals with water and made me drink a whole calabashful of it. It tasted like hell. Then he smeared my body with sticky egg yolks and made me lie down on the floor for twelve whole hours, if not more, while he left to go and eat and, as I heard later, even had a hot afternoon quickie with his youngest wife. Then he returned, tapped me several times with his goat-tail wand, ordered me to get up and told me with all the certainty of his magical powers that nothing bad, no grain of harm, would ever come to me in Europe. All was going to be golden for me there and, though I was going there poor, I would return with wealth and bring honour to Naka. And I, like my mother and all the other villagers, believed him. The night before my departure I couldn't sleep. When I shut my eyes I only dreamt of horrible unclear things, which frightened me. One dream that I vividly remembered the next morning was an unclear scene in a large room somewhere that was filled with thick misty smoke, and in which I saw no one and heard no one till suddenly Akobi's deep-throated laughter suddenly filled the whole room and with it faces of all kinds and sizes that penetrated through the heavy smoke and encircled me. I opened my eyes and never shut them again till I got up to get ready for my agent who was due to pick me up around 7 p.m.

Not many saw me off at the airport. My mother couldn't come because of my two kids whom she felt would be too exhausted to make the trip. My father didn't come because I didn't want him to come so I hadn't formally told him when exactly it was that I was leaving. Only two of my sisters came, clad in snow-white clothes to symbolise the special happy occasion my trip to Europe signified. I wore jeans, the first ever pair of jeans, or indeed trousers for that matter, that I had worn in my whole life. I felt ecstatic about wearing these. They had been given to me, together with the rest of my attire, namely: a sweatshirt, a pullover, Adidas sport shoes and socks. Even though I was sweating profusely in them, since, after all, I was still in Africa, it was a sweat of pride. I was sweating as much from the sweatshirt as from the excitement of being on my way to Europe. When the announcement eventually came through that travellers should get ready to check through emigration, I felt the moisture run down my thighs inside my trousers. The long-awaited moment had come. I hugged my two sisters, then Mama Kiosk who fiercely clutched me tight to her generous bosom and wouldn't let me go till she noticed the rising impatience of the agent. Then I was on my own, walking away from them, following my agent.

We passed through emigration without much trouble. The desk clerk tried to make a small palaver over some vaccination date of my agent's which had long expired, but was expertly tackled with a five-pound note which my agent smartly pushed into the clerk's palm. I saw how the clerk's face lit up and shone when he noticed that the note was no local currency but hard Western currency which, when changed on the black market, would feed him and his family for God knows how long. My agent knew his way about in these things. He travelled regularly between Africa and Europe. Men paid him to smuggle their wives and girlfriends, who had no valid visas, into Europe, a very risky but lucrative business that had rewarded him with a beautiful family house by the seaside in the city's coastal area, four food transport trucks and all the much-worshipped trappings of life à la civilisation: television, radio, fridge – you name it . . . he had it all. He enjoyed this his jet-set life very greatly since, after all, all his to-and-fro tickets were paid for by his customers. Akobi, for instance, had paid him his return trip to Europe, plus of course the cost of his labour. All he had to do was see me through emigration at home and through immigration in East Berlin. So, with the many search clerks behind us, we eventually separated into the respective male and female final body-check cabins. When I emerged to join him, we descended the steps together onto the tarmac to board the airport bus that was to drive us right up to the gangway.

What I felt as we neared the big jumbo jet fast transformed my sweat into shivers and left me trembling with sheer joy. I was travelling to Europe! I wanted to scream and shout to the world about it. When I placed my first foot upon the gangway, I turned my head to take a final look at my people. I waved, even though I was too far away to see any of my sisters, and people waved back, because everybody was simply waving at everybody and all that mattered was that someone waved at someone, it didn't matter who. When I decided that I had waved enough I began my ascent into the plane with no less a feeling than of one going up Heaven's stairway.

The pretty blond stewardess at the doorway smiled at me and said something that I didn't understand, but that too didn't matter. My agent was by me and replied cordially. Then he took my arm and guided me into the vastness of the Aeroflot plane and to my seat. I was still turning my head round and round about because it was the first time I was seeing the inside of a plane. Even though we were still on earth I already felt in the air. Everyone who came in after us I saw because I never took my eyes off the door till the last person came in and the

57

stewardess too came in and the door was shut and we were locked inside this huge flying enclosure. More things were said and demonstrated, none of which I understood. But that didn't matter either. My agent was there and I had nothing to fear. He helped me with my seat belt and told me that we would soon be moving. Then all at once my stomach sank inside me and I realised that we were off Mother Earth, out of reach of Her cuddling arms and were now at the mercy of the skies. Now there was no turning back. I was on my way to the whiteman's land. I was going to see the land that the big doctors and lawyers see, where the Ministers travel with their wives and girlfriends, the land I once thought was so far away and so near Heaven I dared not even think about it. This was the land my feet would step upon before the breaking of another day. And the feeling was great.

The time floated by as we floated too. I spent it sleeping, waking, eating, watching a film I didn't understand and sleeping again. When I woke up I stayed awake till we touched down at the Schönefeld Airport in East Berlin.

Immigration posed no problem at all here and I realised that it was because I had a transit visa even though I had never been to the East German embassy at home. But like I said, my agent knew his job well.

Many with whom we travelled were paying money to some East German official and heading to somewhere. My agent replied, when I asked him why we weren't joining them, that these were also people without West German visas but who got themselves cheap and bad agents. 'They are going to end up in refugee camps,' he added, and laughed terribly. Then I saw that he was staring ahead of us and grinning to an approaching African man who was also smiling and grinning back. This man shook hands vigorously with my agent, then dragged him aside for what I assumed to be consultations. When they rejoined me I asked if Akobi had come to meet us and was told that we were still not through to where Akobi was. I asked again about the many others and I was told that they were going to ask for political asylum. My agent explained it further to me, seeing that I didn't quite understand it: 'They will be put in camps and be compelled into a life that even their bush ancestors never lived.

Your husband thought better of it for you, you know.' He grinned. I don't know why, but something about his grin disconcerted me and it dampened my desire to ask further questions. Then we all three headed to a station where my agent took my passport, and a small clutchbag that the anonymous third man had with him, and disappeared into the toilet. He emerged minutes later, walked straight up to me and gave me a passport. I noticed immediately that it wasn't my passport. This one was older than mine and had many travel stamps in it. But the picture in it looked so very nearly like me that we could have been sisters. I was told that this was what I was going to use for the border into the West.

'In the German people's eyes,' the anonymous third began, 'we niggers all look the same. Black faces, kinky hair, thick lips. We don't fight with them about it. We use it to our benefit.' He laughed cynically.

'But I still don't understand why I must use this passport,' I complained.

'Because this woman whose passport you have has a valid staying permit for West Germany for at least five years, thanks to some poor wretched and destroyed German drug addict she married. And using it from here to West Berlin is like you came from West Berlin to look around East Berlin and you are returning back to West Berlin. Simple. Or do you want to end up in a refugee camp? Oh, if you want to, I can just take you back and put you on one of those buses and you will just have to announce at Checkpoint Charlie that you are fleeing political persecution in your country and want to seek refuge in dear old West Germany. Is that what you want? Don't you want to see your husband?'

'Don't I want to see my husband?' I bellowed, wide-eyed. 'Of course I want to see my husband!' The anonymous third laughed heartily and said, 'Good, then do as we tell you. Show no fear if you are getting checked, or you will betray yourself. Remember, this is your passport. Put that into your head until I give you back your own, is that clear?'

'Yes,' I muttered.

Seeing the apparent trace of worry on my face, he added, 'This is nothing new or something that you should be afraid of. It's just a method that keeps complications at bay. That's all.'

How very right he was. The official who checked me just glanced at my face and at the picture, scurried through the passport and, rather than scrutinising to see the minute differences between my face and that of the person in the picture, seemed more concerned to know why I had married a 'Deutscher' and not an 'Afrikaner' like myself, and whether I was intending to continue living in this their fatherland after my five years expired, and wouldn't it be better for me to return back to Africa? Germany was too cold, didn't I think? As if he was so concerned about how cold or how warm I felt when in truth his only concern was: 'Ach du meine Güte!' Yet another primitive African face come to pollute the oh-so-pure German air and stuff it with probably yet more unwanted brown babies! No wonder my agent and his friend were so damned confident I wouldn't get caught. They were too well-versed in the German mentality. So that just as smoothly as I was promised, I entered the West without needing to proclaim myself a political refugee. But I was still not happy because I had still not seen Akobi. I had thought that he would be missing me just as much as I had missed him and, like me, would be equally impatient to see me too. For who said a lorry-station boiled-eggs-hawker like me didn't know romance? Not only did I know it; I craved and expected it. Events so far had left me so disappointed that I began even to feel it in my teeth. Unable to hold back any longer, I asked again when I would see my husband. 'You will see your husband when you see him,' replied my agent sharply, his patience clearly stretched thin. That put me squarely in my place. I asked no more questions as we drove into town and eventually drew up at some apartment where we were noisily and boisterously received by other Africans who fed us generously. Then we drove to a station. I couldn't make out if it was the same that we first arrived at. Everything just simply looked the same to me, especially the people. The young women with light hair all looked the same to me, just like those with dark hair. So too did the men, kids and old folk. And I thought: one really cannot blame the German police, you know.

60

My agent now left me wholly in the care of the still anonymous third man. As we were now alone with each other, this man introduced himself to me as Osey and said we would be riding by train to Hamburg where my husband lived.

It was night, although I didn't know exactly what time it was. Osey said we had nearly three hours to wait for the train so he bought us bread with strange-looking sausages in it, a kind I had not seen before in my life but which I ate because I was hungry. He said that there was something important I shouldn't ever forget: Germany was the land of six things and six things only: knickerbockers, hunter's huts, sausages, brown bread, beer and Mercedes Benz cars. 'Never forget that,' he reiterated and laughed. Then very unexpectedly he said, 'We have time. We can go and watch a film.' Not waiting for my opinion, he virtually dragged me along.

What a film! I know films. I sold sweets and cigarettes in front of cinema houses back home and many a time ended up with free peeps. But I tell you, this film that Osey took me to go and watch, I concluded with certainty that he was definitely out of his mind. Naturally I understood no word of what it was they talked on the screen but I didn't need to understand German to understand what was going on before my eyes. Osey said before we went into the cinema house that this was his welcome treat for me, a film full of action. So action film it was I had in mind, and expected to see John Wayne, for he was the only popular name I knew from back home. No one talked of action film back home without automatically meaning a John Wayne film. But no! What I saw was not the kind of action I expected. Osey obviously had a different opinion of what an action film was. This action that I saw horrified me and left me sitting in my seat heated up with my mouth wide open. The people on the screen, they were . . . that is to say, they were several men and women all together; about fifteen or so; among them, black women, Africans; and they were doing it there . . . there on the screen! They were actually doing the thing plain plain there on the screen before everybody. And there was no trace of shame or whatever on their faces. Not one bit!

It was a shock for me, my first shock, my first horror. And yet, my first lesson too. It began to dawn on me that I was in a completely new society where the values were different from those at home. Action film at home may mean John Wayne kicking in the air with hands and feet, hopping on and off horses' backs, hallelujahing his cowboy hat in the Western wind and excitedly letting bullets fly at random. Here, action film à la Osey, was raw obscenity. When I told him just that, thinking it would embarrass him, he turned the tables on me, belittling me and reproaching me to leave my primitiveness back home and to start living in civilisation. He asked, even more sarcastically, whether I was maybe too blind to see the two beautiful African women in it who were enjoying the freedom that civilisation offered. Equally sarcastically, I replied that: thank God! I was not so blind and I saw it all . . . in full!!

9

Returning to the waiting room, Osey said we had just fifteen minutes more and could go straight up to the train. People were boarding it, so we boarded it too and went into a compartment in which an elderly lady sat already, very unnaturally frigid in a red hat and grey outfit. We occupied two of the three seats facing her, Osey having nicely greeted her and she having nicely responded, even with a smile, stiff though it was. But once the train started and she apparently realised that she was stuck alone with us two niggers inside the compartment, she started fidgeting nervously, uttering short curt coughs. Osey, noticing this, began to grin, grinned continuously wide and foolish straight into the woman's face. The woman, very evidently uncomfortable now, became so nervous and began to drop things – her tissue, her handbag, her glasses – and Osey continued grinning into her face, wide wide wide. In my ignorance, I just sat there, not understanding what was going on.

We had looked into many compartments before we settled on this one and maybe that should have told me something, but it didn't. Osey went on grinning at the woman, until her lips began to twitch and she started turning red in the face. Then unexpectedly (to me at least) she started to pack her things . . . and Osey grinned on. She folded her newspaper and put it into the bag beside her on the seat. She adjusted the hat on her head, then stood up and removed a grey coat hanging on a hook in a corner and, saying nothing to anyone, snatched a small suitcase from the rack above her, slung her coat over her arm, picked up her handbag and tottered out of the compartment . . . and Osey still grinned on!

'Did I do something?' I asked, baffled.

'You did nothing,' he replied, still grinning.

'Did you do something?'

'I did nothing. I just grinned,' he replied, still grinning.

'So why did she leave?' I queried.

'Because she fears monkey grin,' Osey replied, still grinning.

'Whose monkey grin?'

'My monkey grin,' and he uttered a loud laugh.

'You have a monkey grin?' I asked naively.

'No, but she thinks I have a monkey grin.' He laughed some more, which made me ask, 'And you laugh about it?'

'Should I cry about it?' About the same time our compartment door opened and someone's head peeped inside and asked if the empty seats were free.

'No,' replied Osey, very much to my astonishment, 'our brothers and sisters and father and mother and grandfather and grandmother have gone into the toilet. They will be returning here.' He grinned.

Ah! Osey's grin makes everyone uncomfortable and I guess it did this woman too. She looked at Osey very strangely and then sharply withdrew her head and was gone. Without doubt the picture she carried away with her was that of a grinning African gorilla who was acting strangely in there.

About ten minutes later the door opened again and the conductor entered to check our tickets, which Osey showed him. He stamped them, looked wonderingly at us, gave them back to Osey and was out seconds later, leaving (I guess deliberately) the slide door only half-closed. Osey sprang up and firmly shut it completely. Then he turned to me and grinned yet again, and holy Lord! there was something, this something extra in the grin I didn't like at all. And seconds later my instinct proved right. Still grinning (you'll think he grins more than he breathes) and staring directly into my face he asked in all coolness and casualness, 'Are you wearing something under your sweatshirt?'

'Pardon?' I stammered, hoping that I hadn't heard right.

'What are you wearing under your sweatshirt?' he re-formulated, still betraying no expression.

'A vest,' I replied, perplexed. 'Why?'

'And your jeans?'

'What?' I bellowed.

'Your jeans. What do you have underneath? Or shall I look for you?'

At this point I sprang up in fury. 'What is this, eh? What are these foolish questions you are asking me, eh? Have you maybe forgotten who I am?'

'Of course I haven't forgotten who you are, my dear,' he replied with exaggerated politeness. 'Oh! how can I ever forget who you are, hm!' He giggled. All this left me feeling foolish and uncertain. And confused, too, for the effect my retort had on him was far from what I had hoped or anticipated.

'I'll tell it all to my husband, Osey, you hear; if you don't stop it here and now!!'

'Oh dear,' he drawled, grinning, 'he is my best friend you know, your husband.'

'That alters nothing, Osey,' I blurted out, 'I will still tell him if you don't stop your nonsense here and now! And I don't care if it spoils your friendship! Not one bit, Osey, you hear! I mean it!!'

But Osey's lips only extended into a sly smile as he gave me an 'oh you poor foolish naive thing' look, shrugged indifferently and ordered apathetically 'Sit!' which I did, wiping the cold sweat in my palms onto my jeans and thinking with satisfaction: I have put him in his place. I was soon to find out that this was a grave error, for, without warning, Osey suddenly shoved his hand into my sweatshirt from below, causing me to spring up like I was on fire. I was so baffled and so filled with anger that for a moment all I could do was gasp. Almost immediately afterwards, like one deadly bored by the most uninteresting woman in the world, he said off-handedly, with an arrogant wave of his hand, 'Oh sit down and stop all this monkey drama. Did I eat you?'

There was even a note of anger in his tone; I must say, very much to my stupefaction, since, after all, I felt that I was the one entitled to be angry, not him. I couldn't understand the world any longer. I mean, here was a man openly claiming to be my husband's best friend trying to seduce me, and who was not only bored and angry at my reaction, my threat to report him, but goes out of his way to call it monkey drama! Honestly! I was angry and frustrated. Did Akobi have anything to do with this?

'Did my husband perhaps ask you to do this to me?' I asked him finally. Chuckling arrogantly, he replied, 'Cobby paid me to transport you from East Berlin to Hamburg.'

'Heh, what was that? What is Cobby?'

'Cobby?' he repeated derisively. 'Oh dear! You mean you don't know that too? A-ya-ya-ya-ya,' shaking his head slowly from side to side, 'he also kept that from you? Cobby is your husband Akobi. He changed his name to Cobby because he thinks that sounds more civilised. Actually, I think so too. It's more hip you know. You know hip? Akobi sounds too primitive, too, how shall I say it, too African, yes, too African. Don't you see it that way, too? Which is why he flavoured it with a bit of eh . . . let's say, Europeanism, you get it? Actually, I think he did a good job of it. You think so too, don't you?'

And it was like he was teasing me, deriding me, singing my naivety to my face. As if this turmoil he had created in me was not enough, he resumed, 'Crossing women over the border, Madam Akobi, is not just the passport trick, unless the full fee is paid. Your dear Cobby knows the rules. And he deliberately did not pay the full fee, which makes laying you for free a part of the deal. You get it?'

I stared at him, wide eyed, shocked, not understanding.

'Sit,' he ordered again. Only then did I realise that I was standing. I sat.

'Have no more fear, hm!' he went on. 'You are not a bad-looking chicken, I must say, but you are too green, and such greenness kills my appetite. Maybe next time, another time in the near future after you've received enough coaching and improvement.'

'Improvement?' I howled. 'Coaching? What improvement? What coaching?' And I was hurt more than ever. I needed improvement? I, who was wearing jeans? Adidas canvas shoes?

66

Sweatshirt? My hair Afro-combed? I needed improvement? And coaching?

'What improvement?' I yelled again. 'What coaching?'

But he ignored me. For the rest of the journey, he didn't talk to me. Indeed, he dozed off and left me sitting there feeling idiotic. Only when an announcement burst through the microphones did he open his eyes and tell me to put on my pullover because we had arrived in Hamburg. As I did so, straightening myself up and brushing down my clothes with my nervous fingers, I thought to myself: soon it will be over, this nightmare. Soon you will be out there and in the safe arms of Akobi and everything wil be fine. My third error.

We left the train. Osey, though he had only his clutchbag to carry, still did not help me with my portmanteau, but I told myself not to worry. Akobi would soon materialise and help me with it. As for this Osey, not only was he a foolish man, he hardly even deserved to be called a monkey. He was a gorilla!

We walked through the crowd, encountering a few more Africans, men and women, some of whom Osey greeted, while with others he stopped to exchange words. Then we were out and I was only waiting for Akobi to materialise. And Akobi was still nowhere to be seen. I started growing desperate.

'Is Akobi not here?' I asked eventually, unable to hold back any longer. Osey, as if just opening his lips to answer me was costing him all his life's energy and patience, replied, 'Cobby has no time yet. You will see him tomorrow evening, if luck permits.'

My heart pounded wildly. 'And where will I sleep today?' I asked.

But he ignored me with a rough wave of the hand and headed towards a taxi. We boarded it, me at the back with my portmanteau and Osey in front beside the driver. We drove through seemingly unending broad streets, between shops and office buildings, the kind I had seen many times in films back home. Then Osey said something to the driver. From the moment we had climbed into the taxi I had been wondering what this man was because, with his body like he had gone and baked himself in the sun somewhere, he reminded me of the corrupt Lebanese and Syrians back home who have taken control of trade, running it in a manner that can only be compared with the mafia. Osey told me later that he was a Turk and that there were just as many here as the Lebanese and Syrians back home, but that while the Syrians and Lebanese had made us second-class citizens in our own motherland, the Turks were very much the second-class citizens here. Osey had obviously told this man something very funny because the driver was laughing boisterously and spraying saliva all over, nodding vigorously and casting sly looks at me in his driving mirror. While I was still wondering what it was that Osey had told him, he took a bend, still laughing. Then, unexpectedly, Osey exclaimed, 'Hey look! look there!'

I looked. The driver had deliberately slowed down and was looking too and laughing, like a fat fool. And so too did Osey seem to me. I was the one fighting nausea.

'There are many pretty African women like you here, Mara,' Osey said, chuckling. 'They do what I wanted to do with you in the train, for which you killed my appetite. But for money, not for free like I wanted to do with you or like your husband Akobi did once upon a time with you back home. They are rich, profanely rich, so very rich that they can buy your chief and all of your village!'

Blasphemy, I thought. But he burst into a loud laugh and I stared stupidly back at him, not understanding if he was trying to tell me something or was expecting me to understand something without being told. Then he issued some more directions to the driver who was still laughing and spraying saliva and he took another bend where we were suddenly confronted by a large poster of a ravishingly beautiful white woman, a perfect blond, in a slip, sitting on a stool with legs wide apart, eyes cunningly slanted, tongue calculatingly out and the tip upturned between snow-white teeth, just touching the upper scarlet lip seductively. Further down, the right forefinger just grazed her genitals. I turned my eyes away, so ashamed, so disgusted, so scared and so unsure. Osey, obviously enjoying my dilemma, said, 'This here is the Lord's own anointed street of Hamburg, Mara; His Most Revered Saint Pauli. Here are the cream of Germany's Mary Magdalenes, Mara. And when you receive blessings here, then fear no foe, for then there ain't no Messiah's feet in this whole wide world you cannot wash!' He laughed and laughed and I got more and more confused. I had heard from home of Saint Mary and Saint John, Saint this and Saint that. They were plenty. Schools, churches, streets and avenues, all named after them. And I had always understood them to be some Catholic gods or something like that. But a Saint Pauli in Hamburg and in an area like this filled with wild posters of naked, crimson-lipped women? Did this Saint Pauli have his wires crossed or did he go pinch some forbidden God's salt and get thrown out of Heaven just like his forefather, Lucifer? I didn't understand but I made no inquiries and put no questions to help me understand because I didn't want to understand anything any more.

For one thing had become clear to me: where Osey was concerned, there was nothing pleasant in store for me to understand. Whatever it was he had up his sleeve, only the hope of seeing Akobi soon would keep me going. Every second of that waiting was going to be hell, I knew!

10

The taxi finally put us down before a group of buildings, some tall, some short, some wide, some narrow. Osey told me it was a university campus. I was so unsure of myself, as we walked through the buildings and past a handful of people Osey said were students still on the campus even though it was the vacation. I felt funny, especially when I thought of Osey's claim that the people here called us monkeys. Being so fresh from Africa, I kept thinking that the people probably saw me, even more than Osey, as a monkey in jeans or something like that. So that every little smile on everybody's lips, I misinterpreted to mean a nasty poke at me. And then too there was Osey who still wouldn't help me with my portmanteau and who deliberately saw to it that I didn't level side-by-side with him, vividly reminding me of Akobi and me back home, when he insisted I left home with him mornings while at the same time he didn't want people to see he was walking with me. I was not sure about anything any more. And most definitely not about the village medicine-man with his powder, potions and yolks, and his thousand assurances that only gold and good awaited me here.

We hobbled through and eventually entered one of the tall buildings and went via the stairway to the second floor, then further past a couple of doors before we stopped before a grey one. Osey had a key and he opened it. We entered. It was a small, plain room but, by my standards, very modern. A low single bed with a foam mattress, a carpeted floor, beautiful curtains for the two small windows, an armchair, a table and chair with a table lamp that could rotate on its axis; and a bathroom and toilet which came to my attention when the toilet was flushed, indicating that someone was already in the apartment. Akobi? No! It was another African woman who emerged, hair plaited in tiny rows and hanging long and loose and decorated with what looked like a million tiny beads of all colours. She was tall, with long fingernails painted red, and she wore a tiny gold chain on her ankle.

She greeted me coolly and Osey, whom I noticed to be very much at home here, told her in our language, 'This here is Akobi's bundle.' Bundle? Yes I heard right! Bundle it was he referred to me as. And now, I thought, what next? The woman studied me briefly, with an expression somewhere between pity and helplessness, and said, 'You can sit.' Which I did, in the armchair. It was early in the morning and I was so tired that sleep was what I desperately needed but I didn't trust myself to make it known.

'Hungry?' the woman asked. But before I could open my lips Osey came in with, 'I've bought her food already.'

My luck was that I was in truth not hungry, otherwise I would, I guess, have had to chew my tongue.

Minutes later Osey left the room and the woman said softly, 'I think he is going to try to get your husband.'

Then after a while she said, 'I hear you have a son.'

'Two,' I replied.

'Two?' She seemed surprised. 'I thought one. Your husband said one.'

'The second one was born after he had already left for here,' I said. 'I wrote and told him. Maybe he didn't get it.'

'Na ya,' she shrugged resignedly and gave me that piteous, helpless look again, then turned to the door because Osey was opening it. He entered, gave me a mixed look and called the woman aside for a brief tête-à-tête. Then he turned his attention back to me and said flatly, 'Akobi will come here later on, in the night, but you will still spend the night here.'

Observing his face and listening to his tone, I gave up any thought of probing further. But then, too, I thought: why ask when Akobi himself was coming? The fact that he was coming at all was joyous news enough. Everything else could wait until later.

Then night came, and I sat there with sweaty palms, waiting for Akobi. I waited and waited as I had once waited at home and watched the seconds tick their way into minutes and the minutes into hours and very gradually but very steadily, my hopes faded. At 11.55 p.m. Osey left the room to go call Akobi again. On his return he shook his head from side to side and said, 'Germany is complicated for us people, you know. I can only tell you to be patient. When the right time comes you will see him.'

'He's not coming?' I asked, even though I knew it was precisely that that Osey implied.

'No,' he replied flatly.

The force of an intense disappointment hit me. An ache crept through the veins of my heart and I thought with each new minute that I wouldn't survive the next. When it eventually became clear to me that I might as well retire to bed I asked Osey where I would sleep. I thought maybe there was a mat hidden somewhere under the bed for me to lay out on the floor and sleep on, but he replied, rather jovially, 'Oh, sleep, sleep, go to sleep. You are sleeping on the bed with my wife. I don't sleep here. I am leaving.'

I was baffled. Where was he leaving for? But I was too tired to care. The woman wished me good-night and lent me a night-gown. I got into bed and closed my eyes but didn't go straight to sleep. That was how I came to hear the woman say to Osey things like, 'It's the woman, isn't it? Mama mia, she is a witch-oo!'

But somewhere along the line, sleep eventually overtook me. And when I woke up next morning Osey was truly gone, and his wife was sleeping beside me. I found her to be a really nice woman once Osey had gone and we were alone. She greeted me heartily and directed me about, then, when I had emerged refreshed from the shower, fetched me a steaming hot coffee and fresh bread, with yet more of those strange sausages. For a moment I thought that I could confront her with the talk I had overheard the previous night, but she announced that she had to go out urgently. I was to remain indoors and not to go anywhere until she returned. 'If you are hungry again there's more bread in the bread tin there and more sausages in the fridge. Plus cola, too, those red and white cans,' she added. Then she was gone.

She didn't return till very late at night, getting to ten o'clock. I was feeling so awful from the cans and cans of coke and bread and sausages that I had wrapped myself up in bed. What else was to be expected of an African daughter used to a daily intake of hot chilli and cayenne pepper?

'Sleep, sleep, don't let me disturb you,' was what she whispered when I raised my head to see her as she came in. I even forgot that I had been desperately intending to ask her whether no one here ate hot peppers. What was I doing stuffing myself morning till night with coke and bread and sausages, eh? But the following day was the same. Fortunately, it only lasted till four o'clock in the afternoon, because she returned with roasted chicken plus something that tasted like fried yam, which I learnt was called potatoes; and a bottle of tomato ketchup which she very considerately mixed with chopped onions and ground cayenne pepper. It was my first sensible food in four days.

Somehow, I resigned myself to fate and ceased expecting Akobi. Osey came around 8 p.m. and straightaway got into a fight with his wife, demanding to know from her where she was between 2 p.m. and 4 p.m. and how come she had got back at 4 p.m. and not 2 p.m.; and this was all because I naively and uninvitedly burst in and corrected, 'No, it was 4 p.m. when you came in,' when Osey asked his wife what time she returned and she replied straightaway, '2 p.m.' It was too late for me to undo the harm that I'd done. They got into a fight, him beating her with anything that came to hand: coat hangers, books, cushions, bags, while she unsuccessfully tried to hit him back with one hand, and to shield her face with the other.

It was a funny feeling that I had watching them. I mean, Akobi beat me a lot at home, yes, but somehow I identified beatings like this with home. That African men also beat their wives in Europe somehow didn't fit into my glorious picture of European life. I was in Europe, yes, but I still did not know Europe. I'd stayed indoors all this while and had still not completely got rid of my image of Europe being somewhere near

73

Heaven! And Heaven, unless of course the missionaries were lying, was all singing and dancing and clapping and rejoicing! No beating! I was to learn better.

The beating over, Osey pushed his wife into the bathroom, taking with him the cassette player which they turned very loud . . . and left me wondering, alone in the room.

Osey had so far told me nothing and I too had asked him nothing. So around 10 p.m. I was beginning to yawn, when suddenly there was a loud knock on the door.

'Osey,' I shouted.

No reply. They were still in the bathroom and the music was still playing.

'Osey,' I shouted again, moving nearer to the bathroom.

The music was turned down.

'Osey,' I called. 'Osey, someone is knocking on the door. Shall I open?'

'No, don't!' he shot back hastily. 'I'm coming.' He emerged seconds later, hastily zipping up his trousers, bare from waist up. Prudish and naive though I seemed to be then, I made out fast what it was had been going on in the bathroom.

He walked to the door, flung it open and simultaneously screamed some naughty jokes. With vigorous handshakes and pats on the back, he made way for the visitor into the room. And there he stood . . . my husband, Akobi!

I don't know why, but somehow I used to dream a lot, the times before I was to leave home for here, about my encounter with him after all this while. I used to imagine how he would gather me in his arms and press me to him. Of course, love this romantic never existed between us at home, I knew, but I felt that if he wanted me to join him in Europe, then at least there must be some development in his feelings for me; some change, some affection. Maybe since he'd heard of my sewing lessons with Madam Anaba and heard how I now wore, not cloth, but dresses, and not rubber-tyre slippers, but sandals – maybe he now considered me developed enough for him, appropriate enough to be seen by his side. These used to be my thoughts, my dreams. But seeing him now, the moment he entered, my dream evaporated like a drop of coconut oil on a red-hot slab. Not only did he not look in a hurry to embrace me, he evidently did not expect it of me either. Without any verbal exchange, I knew that the old barrier of the city man and the village woman still existed between us. If I thought I had improved enough to close up that gap, he too had developed some more to widen it further. I no longer plaited my hair, I Afro-combed it. But his hair was no longer kinky like mine. He had done things to it which he himself later described as the 'M.J. look'. His shirt was no more the immaculately starched white one but a fancy silk one tucked into a pair of classy striped grey trousers. Under his arm, a crocodile-skin clutchbag completed it all. And as for the scent which he brought with him into the room, it was as if he had bathed himself in aftershave. His once-rough beard had disappeared. Yes, he now belonged to another world, in which all my newly-won confidence was still not enough to guarantee me an entry. My old complex returned. And when he asked, 'So how are you, eh?' he grinned lewdly, and added, 'I can bet my all that this my most trusted friend Osey here was nice to you,' glancing knowingly at Osey. I shrank inwardly. My plan to tell him all that Osey had done and attempted to do, his rude reaction to my threats, the offensive stare of the Turkish taxi driver, Saint Pauli and all, flooded back in one whoosh and left me feeling nauseous, because now more than ever I felt unsure as to why I was here in this land.

Osey, it soon became clear, wanted to consult with Akobi about something in private. He shouted towards the bathroom, 'Hey, have you dressed or is that your big round bottom still bare?' Then to Akobi, he added, tongue-in-cheek, 'I beat her up just before you came. I beat the sense out of her. Ask your wife. She went somewhere and refused to tell me . . .'

His wife's laughter as she entered the room interrupted him. Akobi joined her in the laughter. Osey didn't. Then the two men disappeared into the bathroom and drew the curtain. Their voices came unclearly through, so it was hard to make out what they were saying. But they remained in there for a while and announced immediately on emerging, 'Mara, there is a lot we ought to talk to you about.'

Neither of them needed to tell me that they were going to

confront me with bad news. When Osey insisted that I sit on the bed first before he began, I knew that I was going to be hurt and disappointed. He was the spokesman. On his order, his wife sat down beside me on the bed. Osey sat on the chair facing us, and Akobi slumped into the armchair, checking and re-checking crumples on his shirt and trousers. The whole scene was to me like a trial in the chief's palace court, back home in Naka.

Osey's wife started cracking her knuckles nervously and almost immediately Osey ordered her sharply to stop it, which she did with a grumble and gathered her hands together into her lap. A whole minute's silence elapsed. Then Osey cleared his throat heavily and began, 'Mara, first we must tell you that life here in Germany for us black people, from Africa especially, is very very hard. In the eyes of the people here, we are several shades too black for their land. And many, not all, but many, don't like us, because for them we are wild things that belong in the jungle. I told you they call us monkeys, didn't I?'

'Yes, you did,' I answered.

'And what do humans do with monkeys?' he asked.

'I don't know,' I replied, awed at what he was aiming at, and asked back, 'what do humans do with monkeys?' I looked so very genuinely aghast that his wife laughed. Osey was about to reproach her when Akobi also laughed. So Osey held back and said with a grin, 'Okay, Mara, let me put it this way. One or two monkeys about the civilised man's house are acceptable, but when the monkeys send for their long line of relatives and friends, the "civilised" house owner begins to react. He is prepared to tolerate one or two monkeys about his house, even be kind to them to show what a good heart he has. But when the monkeys too get taken in by his pseudo-kindness and, encouraged by it, send for the others, the "civilised" man shows his real face. And it's almost never a pleasant face, Mara. Do you get me?'

After a long pause I replied, simply, 'No.' And I meant it. It was all a bit too philosophical for me.

'Okay,' resumed Osey, 'it is like this: the German people, or at least those who represent them, don't want too many of us here in their country, so they do all they can to make things very difficult for us, so that we will feel humiliated and think of

76

returning to our homeland as a palatable alternative. Do you understand?'

I didn't reply.

'For instance,' he went on, 'that was why I made you use someone else's passport to come here. You understand?'

'Yes,' I replied.

'Because, otherwise, you would probably have been sent back by the police on the next plane. But with this passport, you had no such problem. And you know why?'

'No,' I answered.

'Good,' he said, with a vigorous nod, 'then I'll tell you why. This woman whose passport you used, she has permission to live here in Germany. And you know why? Because she is married to a German man. You understand?'

My heart's tempo quickened. I didn't reply. He resumed anyway.

'Look, Mara, Akobi has permission to live here. And me too. My wife came about nine months ago and is working to get plenty money to marry a German man so that she too will have no problem living here. You understand? We don't do it because we want to. We do it because we have to. It is the only way out for us to live here. And why do we have to live here? Not because we want to, Mara. You yourself will find out soon. But because many of us have sold our properties and inheritance and taken money from every member of our family just to come here to work in the factories we heard at home were in abundance and needing workers. You have to come here to know that it is not true. But we have already taken all this plenty money from back home. So how do we return home with empty hands? We must find the money somehow, fair or foul. And anyway, who will believe you at home if you return and tell them that there is no work, and that German people too are themselves without jobs? You will be accused of being a born failure, or they will say that you offended the gods and the ancestors, and that you are trying to justify your shame by dissuading other people from going to Europe to try their luck. Do you understand me now?'

I must confess that I still didn't quite understand in full, but I was overwhelmingly impressed with Osey. He was a chameleon.

I didn't know that this Osey that I hated so much, this arrogant wife beater, had any sense inside his head. Now I knew that he did. Akobi, who had remained silent all this while, now came in and said, 'Osey, now you've preached enough. Explain to her now the difference between her situation and your wife's.'

And Osey, obviously not too pleased about being told to cut short his sermon, replied irritably, 'Yes, but first things first. She must be prepared for it.' Then he turned to me and resumed, 'You see, my wife here, she is working hard now to save plenty money to pay a German man to marry her . . .' My face clouded so much that he had hastily to seek a better presentation, for whoever heard of a woman in Africa working hard to save plenty money to pay a man to marry her?

'. . . or better still,' he resumed, 'you see, my wife here, she is my wife and she loves me. And this German man that she will marry, she doesn't love him and he too doesn't love her. But they will marry. And it will only be on paper, official, that they are married. You get me? Privately, they won't do things together like two people who are married. You understand? And that is the reason why she has to pay him . . .'

'And the man,' I interrupted. 'Whom does he love?' I surprised myself that I had the guts to ask a question. But this Osey talking here was different in a significant way from the Osey before now. This new Osey here, I realised, could be questioned.

'This man loves a certain white powder that makes you high and is very expensive and . . .'

'Return to the subject, Osey,' Akobi interrupted impatiently, 'she doesn't understand all this "high" thing anyway.'

And Osey said, 'Yes, so you see, Mara, Akobi and I, when we came, we didn't have any money to pay some woman to marry us. You get what I am trying to say? So we had to marry seriously . . . that is to say, for false love. Like we loved the women, you get me? Even though we don't love them. You understand?'

I didn't, and I said so. That irritated Akobi.

'It is this,' he came in impatiently in a no-nonsense tone. Turning briefly to Osey, he said to him, 'Osey, let me tell her straight and direct. Mara, I have married a German woman. That was what Osey was trying to tell you all this while . . .'

78

'Your second wife?' I asked weakly. 'You have taken on a second wife and you didn't tell my family back home?' Our tradition demanded this. It was a sign of respect to the first wife and her family. When a man took on a second wife without informing the first wife or her family, it showed an indifference towards his in-laws, which in itself was considered disrespectful and humiliating.

But Akobi butted in, even more irritated and replied, 'Mara, call it what you like, but polygamy here is not like polygamy at home. Here, polygamy is a crime – they call bigamy. And I can go to prison for it, you understand?'

'No, I don't,' I replied. 'Why should a man go to prison because he has taken a second wife?' I was genuinely baffled.

'Why? I don't know why!!' Akobi virtually screamed, completely at an end with his nerves and patience. 'Look,' he resumed, 'it's quite simple. Here, one man one wife: that is the law. If a man takes more than one wife, he has broken the law. And if you break a law, you pay or go to prison. That is why I can't tell my wife . . . my German wife, I mean, that I have another wife. You understand?'

'No,' I replied, and Akobi sighed and fell back in the armchair as if to imply: God! I give up! And here it was that Osey's wife now came in for the first time, having remained quiet all this while. 'Look,' she began, 'it is this. Akobi has married a German woman here so that he can live here long enough in peace to be able to make plenty money and repay all the money he took from home to come here. He has also brought you here, don't forget. And that too costs money. So he can't tell his wife that you too are his wife. You get it now? So you will go and live with them, but as his sister and not as his wife. You understand?'

'But I'm not his sister!' I protested.

'No. But you are from now on,' she said, 'and will have to continue to be until it is no longer necessary, unless you want to find yourself back in Naka tomorrow. Do you?'

Foolish question! Who would want to, in my position? I didn't reply.

She went on, 'Look, it is the same with me and Osey. We are very happy. I live here and at my other place and he lives with his wife in town. She believes that I am his sister, and we get on fine. No problem. Look, even this nightgown I lent you, it was she who gave it to me. Ah, she gives me plenty things: lipstick, eyeshadow, pants, this, that. And in return I go on enduring her. I just shut my eyes to our rivalry and then it is simple. I don't see why it should be difficult for you to do so. What would you have done if you were at home and Akobi had taken a second wife?'

'Then the second wife would have acknowledged me as the first wife, and therefore the senior wife, and given me the due respect,' I replied.

'And who says his German wife won't give you respect?' she asked.

'As her senior rival?' I asked in a sarcastic tone.

She obviously didn't like my challenge too much. 'Look,' she shot in, 'didn't your mother have a rival?' she asked sharply.

'Am I my mother?' I retorted, gradually becoming aware that I could assert my opinion and get away with it, and even ask relatively daring questions I definitely wouldn't have had the guts to ask some time ago. If this allowance for audacity was part and parcel of civilisation, then it probably wasn't as bad as I thought it was after watching that film with Osey in Berlin. I was enjoying it.

'Sister,' Osey's wife came in again, this time a bit reservedly, 'it is not much different from our marriage situation at home. It's just that here, instead of the German wife knowing that you are her rival, she must by all means believe that you are his sister. That is all.'

'Yes,' Osey said, ending his long silence, 'and even with you, you must be glad that Akobi can take you to go and live with him. My wife here didn't have that luck when she came. I tell you, Mara, you will be so happy that you won't even care any longer about playing the sister role, because they have everything in the apartment, Mara, everything: fridge, stove, sofa, carpet, record player, cassette player, radio, television! Ah, plenty plenty things. You will see for your own self . . .'

'It is not difficult,' Akobi agreed. And I realised that they hadn't expected that I would put up any resistance and ask the many questions I shot at them. Akobi was over-confident that I was the Mara of back home who said yes and bowed to every order without question. He saw now that he shouldn't have been so confident. Since so much depended on me, I could easily give the game away and it wouldn't be only me who would suffer the consequences.

Akobi was now trying to be cautious with me. And anyway, if I didn't go along with what they were demanding of me, what other alternative did I have? So I said nothing more. I just decided to sit there and let them go on planning my fate for me.

'He has already told her of your coming, so it is no problem,' said Osey. Then, turning to Akobi, he asked, 'What did she say when you told her?'

'Oh, what could she say?' replied Akobi pompously. 'I told her straight and simple that if she loves me then she must accept my sister too.'

'Only that?' asked Osey's wife, amazed.

'Well,' drawled Akobi arrogantly, 'then I frightened her a little that if she didn't accept my sister now, she should know too that my family back home would not accept her when we emigrate to Africa.'

'A one-one draw?' asked Osey with a chuckle.

'Something like that,' Akobi agreed. 'You know how she dreams of a life in Africa: warm weather, palm trees, fresh fruits, and ten thousand bambinis attending to her wishes.'

'And when are you going?' asked Osey's wife with a laugh.

'She wants us to go in a year's time,' Akobi replied.

'I thought it was three,' said Osey.

'Yes, that was three months ago. She cut it down to two and then to one. Each time someone calls her "du Negerfrau" she cuts it down. But I was able to convince her to make it two years,' Akobi replied with a laugh.

'And when the two years come?' asked Osey.

'Oh, then I'll convince her that we'll make it in yet another two. Simple.'

He laughed. So that although I had intended to remain quiet I broke the silence to ask, 'But then one day you will have to take her, won't you?'

Because I was already thinking what would happen. Once a sister always a sister. So my sister role would continue even at home if we all three returned. And since we would have to keep this act a secret from my family and from his family and from all Naka, I would remain stuck with them. She would continue seeing in me the oh-so-loyal sister-in-law and old-maid-sister of her husband. As to what would happen to our two sons, I dared not imagine. But to my question, Akobi replied sharply, 'Don't ask naive questions. Before the time comes when I will no longer be able to convince her to let us postpone our trip to Africa, I'll already have made enough and bought all that I came here for and be living already in my fully-furnished bungalow back in Africa.'

I noticed starkly that he hadn't said in OUR fully-furnished bungalow.

11

The schooling and discussion ended after midnight on the assumption that I had understood everything and agreed with everything. All that was left now was to prove how good an actress I was.

Akobi said that he had told his wife he would be home by midnight and must be getting on his way or she would make trouble with him. Osey, too, said that he had promised to be back by 1 a.m. at the latest, but he never kept his promises, which his wife knew.

Akobi, though, was obviously intending to keep his promise. But the moment he sprang up, just when I thought the worst was over, Osey, back to his old self again, baring his teeth and gums in a gorilla-like grin, nudged Akobi in the ribs and uttered, 'You don't want to tell me you are not going to have a quick welcome one with her before you leave, Akobi? Her appetite is already whetted, I'm sure. We were in there at it when you came, you know,' he said, chuckling like an idiot.

As for Akobi's reaction, I could as well have been a four-penny whore. Without a word he got up, picked up the cassette player, switched it on loud and with just a slight nod of the head towards the bathroom, beckoned me to come and receive my welcome dose. I don't know why I obeyed him and got up at all but I did, drained of all dignity, filled with abhorrence, and tottered behind him into the bathroom, to the chuckles of Osey and his wife. Once inside, he drew the plastic curtain. Then, very rigidly and businesslike, ordered as loud as the loud music would allow, 'Remove it quick quick,' pointing to my trousers.

By the time I had got out of them he too had got his trousers down to his knees. Emanating an aura of no-nonsense, time-is-too-precious-to-waste-on-you, he signalled with his right forefinger that I should kneel; which I did, still in my sweatshirt. Then he took my jeans, spread them on the bathroom floor, and knelt down. I felt him enter me from behind and the next second he was out of me again and demanding hastily to know whether I had taken something against pregnancy. When I replied that I hadn't, I heard him curse impatiently, then lower the radio and shout to Osey to bring him one rubber please! I heard Osey grumble and his wife chuckle. Seconds later Osey's hand poked through the side of the curtain and handed a condom to Akobi. Then he peeped through and laughed out loud and said to me, 'You look like you're waiting to grind your mother's millet for her, Mara.' An expensive joke at my kneeling position, naked from waist down, my bare bottom exposed.

I knew that Osey was not to be blamed. I made a ridiculous sight in that posture. My thoughts were curtailed when I felt the sudden sharp pain of Akobi's entry in me. He was brutal and over-fast with me, fast like he was reluctantly performing a duty, something he wouldn't have done if he had his way, but which he must because he must. And then he was up and I was still kneeling there, very much in pain because what he did to me was a clear case of domestic rape.

Then he shouted to Osey to ask if they were over with theirs. Osey shouted back that he should come out into the room and stop pretending to be the holy carpenter Joseph. Only later did I understand this because with the cassette now turned very low I was able to hear Osey and his wife still at it, or at least, the final bits and pieces. I was hearing this in the bathroom alone while Akobi was in the room with them. And since I heard no horrified screams from either the wife or Osey, I concluded that this wasn't the first time Akobi was seeing Osey's wife naked or the two of them having sex together; which, I concluded, explained the arrogance with which Osey tried to seduce me in the train.

I stood up and was putting on my underpants when Akobi drew

open the curtain, not caring at all about Osey, who was standing directly behind him, seeing my nakedness, his eyes fixed on my genital area. 'I'll be here to pick you up at 4 p.m. tomorrow. So be ready and waiting,' he said. Then he turned and was gone.

I emerged from the bathroom feeling embarrassed and ashamed. I kept my eyes down.

'You don't need to feel ashamed, Mara,' Osey's wife said unexpectedly. I was surprised. Firstly, because she had noticed that this whole careless sex show was a fraction too new and too much for me; and secondly, because the tone in which she spoke was totally different from what I was used to all these days I had been living with her. This tone was somehow big-sisterly. So I lifted up my head and my eyes fell upon her face and I said meekly, 'It's the first time he's done it with me within the hearing distance of others. And I don't like it.'

She stood there for a while, staring at me. Then she rushed to me and gathered me in her arms. 'Oh Mara, oh my God,' she said, and just continued holding me close.

'I don't like it,' I repeated, and burst into the desperate sobs that had been stuck in my chest.

She continued to hold me close and when my sobs gradually died down, led me to the bed. We both sat there for a while in complete silence. Then, suddenly, I asked her, 'Are you happy? Truly happy? The way things are? The situation you are in?'

She allowed time to elapse. Then she replied simply, 'I don't know, Mara. I am not that sad but I am not that happy either. I love Osey, you know. With us, our families didn't fix us together. We fixed ourselves together, so we are a bit different from you and Akobi. Osey and I, we met at a village durbar. We found out that we both lived in the city so we arranged to meet again when we returned. We met and continued to date each other until we discovered ourselves and eventually slept with each other. Osey had chosen no wife then, but my family had eyes on a man as husband for me. Osey and I just had the luck that the family of the husband chosen for me had by then still not come to formally sit down with my family. Otherwise I would probably have never got married to Osey and would not be here. You ask if I am happy with the situation as it is. Hm. I do miss little things, you know; little wifely things, like washing and ironing his shirts, like going to bed with him, sleeping beside him all the night through and waking up in the morning with him beside me. Like waiting at home for him and worrying my head about when he would at long last come home and eat the food I've cooked for him. You know, petty things like that.' She chuckled sadly. 'But it's a situation I have to survive with. And you too must, Mara. It's the only survival open to us.'

I said nothing.

'It must be much easier for you, Mara, if you don't love Akobi,' she resumed. 'Or do you love him?'

'I don't know,' I replied. 'I don't know what it is to love a man. I never learnt it because I wasn't taught. I never experienced it because I never got the chance to love before this marriage was arranged with Akobi. I only know that a girl grows up, is given to a man by her parents and she has to please the man, serve him and obey him and bear him plenty children. Is that love?'

'No,' she replied, laughing, 'love is something that you feel. You feel it. Do you feel anything for him?'

'Like what?' I asked.

'Like . . . like, say . . . attachment. Like, say, desire to sleep with him and touch him and be by him all the time. Do you feel that?'

'I don't know,' I replied. 'Attachment? I think I feel a bit of it for him, yes. Sleep with him? Hm. I don't know. After this that he did to me in the bathroom? Hm. When he married me, I thought all the time that he slept with me that he was doing it so that I would bear him a son. But when I got pregnant he wasn't happy about it at all. So I don't know why he slept with me.'

'He is a man, Mara, and when he has a risen penis he will sleep with anything that has a vagina and leave the regret for later,' said Osey's wife. 'But here in the bathroom, he didn't sleep with you to let you bear him a son. Otherwise he wouldn't have called for the condom. So he slept with you for the same reason that he used to sleep with you at home.'

'Duty,' I said thoughtfully, 'that was why he did it. But I don't understand why, if it was duty, he got excited at all in the first

86

place and his penis rose at all. Both at home and here. Why did he do it with me if he didn't want to? Because Osey said he must?'

'Maybe, maybe not. How did he make it with you?'

'How did he make it with me?' I asked, my face hot with shame.

'Yes,' she replied, 'don't feel ashamed, Mara. Tell me. We are alone here.'

'Well,' I stammered, 'he made it with me like . . . well . . . like it is made. How else?'

'Yes, Mara, of course he made it with you like it is made. But I want to see if he did it with you because Osey suggested it, or if he did because in spite of feeling that it is a duty he has to fulfil, he also wanted to do it with you. So be honest with me. How did he get his thing hard? Did you do it for him?'

I was, to say the least, flabbergasted. 'Did what?' I exclaimed at the top of my voice.

'Make his thing hard for him! Did you make it hard for him before he actually did it with you?'

'I never make his thing hard for him!' I retorted. 'Akobi always makes his thing hard himself!'

'You've never touched it before? You mean, he's never made you touch his thing before?'

'No!' I howled. 'No! No! No! And I don't want to talk with you about it again, please. Please!' I turned and got into the bed and covered myself, still in my jeans and all.

She got up and went to the toilet. On her return, she too climbed into bed. I tried to sleep but couldn't. She too obstinately refused to start any talk again. But our conversation was ripping my thoughts apart and I was craving to talk. Eventually I couldn't hold out any longer.

'Do you make Osey's thing hard for him before he sleeps with you?' I asked.

'Always,' she replied with closed eyes.

'How?' I queried.

'You won't understand it if it's not something you have done before.'

'How?' I repeated, ignoring what she had just said.

'I rub it in my hands or . . . ah, forget it, Mara. You won't understand!'

'Or what?' I persisted.

'Or put it in my mouth!'

'Your what?' I howled like a crazy dog and the next moment I was out of bed and rushing to the bathroom. I don't know why. I guess I just thought that I should throw up, but nothing came. I returned to the bed.

'Aren't you going to change into a nightgown?' she asked.

I got up and changed and got back into the bed.

'You are green, Mara,' she said at last.

'Mama Kiosk said that too,' I replied sarcastically. 'And Osey too.'

'Who is Mama Kiosk?' she asked. I told her.

'Were you never at school, Mara?' she asked.

'No,' I replied, 'were you?'

'Till Form Two,' she answered. 'I gave up before I could get my Middle School certificate.'

'Osey said that this place is a university,' I began. 'How come you live in a university?'

'It's just temporary. I'll move out when the university re-opens,' she replied. 'I don't live here as such. This room was hired out to us by a German student who has an African girlfriend. But their affair is different. As for them, it is true love that they have for one another. And the woman, too, she is a proper lady. She has been to school plenty and is now learning here. Osey told the German student that his sister was coming for a short visit from Stuttgart and he gave him his key for a few Deutschmarks. But I must be out before he returns because even though he knows that I am Osey's 'sister', he knows too that I don't live in Stuttgart. Then there is his girlfriend, his African girlfriend, who is very unsympathetic towards us. She carries herself as if she is better than us, if you know what I mean. But I think that the real reason behind her attitude is that she knows that I am in truth Osey's wife, pretending to be his sister, and yet she is unable to tell her boyfriend since it will mean betraying her fellow Africans. She dislikes this, so she refuses to speak with us.'

'And where is she now? Where does she live?'

'She lives here, too, just like her boyfriend, but they have travelled together somewhere, Spain or somewhere like that. Anyway, Osey made the whole arrangement so I just depend on him and wait. If he comes here tomorrow and says I must get ready to leave, then I know that they are coming back and I must get ready to leave.'

'What if in truth they are not coming back but Osey just wants you to leave here for some other reason he can't tell you? Can you know?' I asked.

She turned sharply to face me and stared at me, her face slowly clouding like one suddenly confronted with a stark possibility she had never before considered. Then she said, 'No, I can't know,' and continued to stare at me.

After a while, like someone reluctantly admitting for the first time some hard unpleasant fact of life, she said, 'Mara, our life here is very hard, you know. But how can I return home empty-handed? It was Osey who made all the arrangements for me to come here. My brothers and my family only contributed to my fare. And you know the plenty money that goes into the passport. I came here full of hope and found that here, too, I have to continue depending wholly on Osey. He makes every arrangement and simply gives me orders. Even the money that I make, he controls it. I can't buy anything without his consent, not even for my own mother at home.'

'You work?' I asked.

'If what I do can be called work, then yes, I work.'

'Where do you work? What do you do?' I asked.

'I can't tell you. Osey strictly forbids me to.'

'Please,' I begged. 'I won't tell him you told me.'

'No,' she replied firmly. And I knew that she wouldn't tell me unless Osey ordered her to do so.

She looked at the time and exclaimed, 'My God! it's getting to four!'

'Four in the morning?'

'Were you thinking of four in the afternoon?' And we both laughed.

Then I said, 'Have you noticed that I still don't know your name?'

'Vivian,' she said.

I said, 'Vivian, who taught you to rub Osey's thing in your hands and put it in your mouth?'

'No one,' she said, then added as an afterthought, 'or maybe someone did, but I don't remember.' She turned her head away.

I continued lying there beside her; and I thought a lot about me and her. She was a helpless woman who, without her Osey, could move neither to left nor right. And she would probably even stop breathing if Osey ordered her to. She was like me. Our men brought us here and we were at their mercy.

It was simpler those days at home when in my faded clothes and lorry-tyre slippers I had to pretend before Akobi's working colleagues at the bus stop that I wasn't his wife. But now it was not as simple as that because I wouldn't for anything in the world wear those faded clothes and tyre slippers and pretend not to be his wife just to help him keep his head high. There was a change going on inside me, and Akobi was not seeing it and was still handling me like the poor lowly wife of yesterday. At the same time he was asking me to pretend to be something that I wasn't. And all this in the presence and under the watchful eye of the keen observer – his wife, my rival.

My husband Akobi didn't consider me sensitive and intelligent enough to understand and feel this emotional burden he was placing on me. If he thought me so numb, dumb and naive that he could take my feelings and emotions for granted, then how come at the same time he assumed me capable of convincingly playing this sister role on which his whole fate depended?

12

Four o'clock next day, just as he had promised, Akobi arrived to pick me up. He was in a hurry. Just a hasty hello to Vivian and a message that Osey would be coming to her later, and he asked if I was ready. I was. Wasting no second more, he took the lead out of the room and left me to trail behind him, dragging my portmanteau along, for like Osey, he did not help me carry it. Out of the room and out of the building, through the throng of parked cars and bicycles, we soon emerged onto the street.

My eyes first fell on a red Volkswagon Passat parked at the other end. His car? How were we going to go to his home? On foot? By bus? Train? Or by car? We crossed the road and walked past the Passat and past a couple more cars; then finally stopped beside a gleaming metallic blue Honda Accord. This was his car.

He moved to the boot, unlocked and opened it; and I, sideways from behind him, lifted my portmanteau, ready to place it inside . . . and shrank back from his unexpected cry that rang suddenly from his throat, 'Hey, hey, hey, hey, Mara, gently, hey, gently, woman, okay? This here that you see is called a car. Not only a new car but a very expensive car, too. I won't be pleased if your portmanteau scratches it, okay?'

'The man who sold it to mother said it was leather,' I protested, wanting to imply that leather portmanteaus don't scratch new cars. But he had a ready answer.

'It is leather and metal,' he retorted sharply. 'Or can't you see?' He pointed accusingly at the two locks.

I said nothing more. And not that gently, he snatched the

portmanteau from me, then placed it with extreme care inside the boot. Then he walked to the steering side of the car and said to me, 'There are too many things in the front. Sit in the back.'

There were several plastic bags and papers and other things piled up on the front passenger seat. So I complied obediently. The moment I was seated he opened a locker in the front, removed a yellow duster, got out of the car and dusted something (or maybe nothing) off the side door through which I had just got in, climbed back inside, replaced the duster, and started the car. I was amazed.

Was he provoking me or was he sick? I decided it couldn't be the first. Why should he desire to provoke me? For what? So it must be the second. And it got me so nervous that I sat in there at the back like I was in a death chair; straight, rigid and tense, not trusting myself to touch anything or even shift an inch from where I was seated, just in case Akobi should come spraying insecticide there.

I got the impression that the car was his fetish. He worshipped it like his father worshipped his coffins. And one did not tamper with another's fetish. He wound his way expertly through the wide streets of Hamburg and finally approached an old red-brick building in front of which he stopped, turned off the engine and began removing the bags and papers beside him on the front seat and passing them to me in the back to place beside me. Then, front seat cleared, we remained sitting in the car. What we were doing there, he didn't tell me. Whether it was there that he lived, I didn't know. We just sat there, silently. After about fifteen minutes, during which he looked at his watch more than twenty times, he got out, saying nothing to me, and walked into a nearby telephone booth where I saw him make a call and speak and laugh a great deal. When he returned to the car he remained outside it, leaning against the bonnet. Seconds later, I saw a young white lady approach him. I guessed she came from the brick building. She was smiling broadly and he was grinning back. As she neared him she stretched out both arms to him. He took them, drew her closer to him and kissed her on both cheeks. They talked briefly in German. Then the woman bent and looked at me in the car, smiling still. I didn't know what kind of reaction was expected of me so I grinned foolishly back at her. Was this his wife? Was it here that my sister role began? Then I saw her signalling to me to roll down the car window. And I began fidgeting with handles and knobs whose functions I neither knew nor understood. Not only did I not know which opened what, but was rendered even more nervous with the fear of inflicting some harm through my ignorance on this Akobi's fetish. That confused me even more for I didn't dare to think of the consequences I would bring upon myself if I damaged the car. And when I looked at his face I could see that not only was he worried about the damage I might inflict but was also irritated by what he saw as my stupidity. Only when further fidgetings still did not help me open the window did he get in the front and snappily tell me what to do.

The white lady, now laughing, first put her head through to say hello, then her hand, to shake mine, all the time smiling in a friendly way. She went on to say a couple more sentences in German which I naturally did not understand, so I stared at her like a fool, which irritated Akobi even more. In that same snappy tone (though he obviously was trying to control himself and to play it down to avoid detection by the white lady), he told me, with a stiff grin, 'She is asking you how you are, and says welcome to Germany.'

So I grinned wider back at her. I should have said 'thank you', I knew; but what was 'thank you' in German? I did not know.

She turned back to Akobi and they talked a little more before they repeated their kissing ritual, and then she walked away, waving all the while. Then Akobi got in and said brusquely, 'You see? My wife's already gone because I came to pick you up and got here late. Now you see?' As though it was me who had said to pick me up at four o'clock. And as though I wasn't ready when he came. What was this blaming me because his wife was gone? And who was I?

He started the car. The front seat was now empty but he still left me sitting in the back. During the whole drive he spoke no word to me.

We drove for another twenty-five minutes or so past several buildings, two bus stops and a church before we stopped in front of a clutter of very tall apartment houses and got out. Akobi opened the boot and I thought he meant me to take out my portmanteau since after all it was me who dragged it all the time when it needed dragging. So it was only natural for me to assume that I was being expected to pick it up, with him looking on idly and commanding here and there what I should and should not do to avoid scratching this fetish car of his. But to my utter bewilderment, when I made to pick it up, he roughly brushed me aside and took hold of it himself. I looked at him in awe, and thought: he is intending to carry it . . . and saw that indeed he was already carrying it and moving away. What had suddenly come over him? I followed him.

We went round the side of the tall building and entered through the glass door. Then we went up the stairs to the second floor where we stopped before the second door from the left. There were five doors altogther.

Now Akobi took out his key and made to insert it in the lock, and this was when the full reality of my impending role dawned on me.

'What shall I do when we enter and there she is facing me?' I asked nervously.

Akobi turned sharply to face me, so sharply that for a moment I thought he was going to hit me. I could see that he too was dead nervous for, after all, if one slip from me could give the whole game away, I didn't yet know what I would be seeing, but as sure as night and day I knew what Akobi would be seeing: red! And that was why he was as nervous as me.

'You must pull yourself together, Mara. Pull yourself together, woman! You hear me?' he hissed angrily at me, his eyebrows furrowed.

Pull yourself together, Mara? Pull yourself together, woman? I looked back at him, with my portmanteau in his trembling hands, and I so much wanted to laugh. If anyone needed to pull himself together, it was him! But I stared back, aloof, and he went ahead and opened the door.

'Gitte,' he called out the moment we stepped inside, and promptly received his echo back.

'Gitte,' he called again. And yet again, his echo. Then still unconsciously carrying my portmanteau, he dashed hastily about the apartment, peeping through one door after another, all the time calling Gitte. The kitchen, the bedroom, the bathroom. Back in the living room, he sighed dejectedly, shrugged his shoulders, then suddenly remembering that he was still holding my portmanteau, furiously let it fall, giving it an angry, scornful look. Then he growled, sighed, growled again and cast another scornful look at my portmanteau and then at me. He muttered something I could only guess to be a curse. All the better that portmanteaus neither hear nor see nor feel for, I suspected then, that he had carried it for me this once only because he thought that Gitte was home and would probably be watching us from the balcony or the bedroom. So this whole drama of the caring big brother playing gentleman to his little sister was for Gitte's sake. Seeing that his labour had all been for nothing, he was very sour, because Akobi does nothing for nothing, or at least, hates doing something for nothing.

I wanted to sit but I feared him probably screaming at me to hop off up and not dirty his couch. So I thought it better to stand. Let's see if he would come scowling at me, telling me to get my feet off his carpet before they made it dirty! He had just turned and was heading back once again into the bedroom when we both heard what we had been expecting but fearing – the key turned in the door.

'Pull yourself together!' he hissed again.

Then the door opened! And there she was: Gitte. And what a picture!

Shoulder-length auburn hair and a short stubby fat body concealed in a grey woollen skirt, a dark green sweatshirt and black cowboy boots. So this was Gitte!

Somehow, I had always had in my mind the idea that all white women were tall, slim, long-legged and blonde, with sparkling blue eyes and long red lacquered nails, just like in the films I had seen back home. But this my husband Akobi's Gitte, she was anything but this image. I wondered if Akobi's eyes had been dimmed with egg yolk or whether the likes of Gitte were the only ones available for black African men.

He was by her side in a flash, but it wasn't at all a cordial reception that she gave him. I think that she was angry because he was late in coming to pick her up because, right before my eyes, they began exchanging sharp words in German, none of which I understood. Then, somewhere along the line, Gitte must have issued an order to Akobi because I saw him nod obediently as she suddenly swerved round and thumped her way furiously towards the bedroom. He tottered behind her without a glance at me. Neither of them, all this while, seemed to have remembered that I was in the room.

From the bedroom I could hear their arguing voices. Then gradually the noise began to die down until eventually there were just low mutters and then complete silence. Even though they stayed in there for about another twenty minutes or so, I remained standing in the living room, still not trusting myself to sit. At last Akobi emerged, subdued and grinning foolishly. But there was a desperate fury in his eyes and I saw it all too clearly. Gitte had belittled him before my eyes and that had brutally dented his ego. Yet the moment he heard movement behind the bedroom door, indicating that Gitte was about to swing open the door and join us in the living room, Akobi was once more his old commanding self, wiping the grin off his face.

'Don't make your face like that woman! Don't you know that she is already a little suspicious? I don't want any more trouble, you hear! Gather yourself together and smile, Mara. Smile, smile, smile at her!'

I honestly don't know what else Akobi would have commanded me to do if Gitte hadn't at long last (thank God!) emerged from the bedroom, a completely different person, because now she was smiling broadly at me. She approached me and gave me her hand and said, 'Willkommen!'

From the corner of my eyes I observed Akobi look on us with a really foolish grin. I could bet my neck on it that he was congratulating himself on what a fine job he had done, which probably had to do with whatever it was he had said or done to her behind the bedroom door. To my surprise Gitte held out something in her hand for me. It was a ring.

'Für mein schlectes Benehmen,' she said.

Like an excited peacock, Akobi, obviously feeling relieved,

burst in to translate that she was presenting me with the ring as an apology for her earlier behaviour towards me. So relieved was he that he went on to tell me that the ring was silver. 'Pure silver!' he bubbled on, 'Gitte ordered it from a catalogue before she realised that she was allergic to silver.'

I took the ring and thanked Gitte with a low bow. But she unexpectedly grasped me by the shoulders and kissed me in a sisterly way on both cheeks. That moved me and filled me with guilt. How long could I go on cheating on her as her sister-in-law if she continued being so sisterly towards me?

We all sat down. She asked if I was thirsty and I said I was. She got up and disappeared into the kitchen and returned with a soft drink for me. She asked if I was hungry. I said I wasn't . . . after a stolen glance at Akobi, as I very definitely was. He must have noticed my uncertainty because he exclaimed almost immediately, 'You are not hungry?'

Then he turned and spoke to Gitte. I knew by his manner and tone what he must be saying. 'Don't mind her, Gitte. She is hungry but is too shy to say it. African complex.' He was obviously expecting Gitte to say, oh, okay, and then get up again and disappear into the kitchen to prepare something for me. But Gitte responded reproachfully and gestured towards the kitchen. To this, Akobi got up lamely and went into the kitchen

My mouth fell open. I was shocked. Akobi to cook for me? The thought filled me with such worry that I issued another feeble protest even though my stomach was growling. However, Gitte indicated that *she* was hungry and wanted to eat with me.

So Akobi, this my own dear husband Akobi who back home used to reproach me if I was a minute late with his food; who many a time landed me knocks on my forehead with his knuckles if I fetched him too little or too much water in the bowl for him to wash his hands before and after eating; this my very own Akobi it was who, upon his white wife's commands, trotted into the kitchen. Seconds later, the clattering of pans and spoons told me that he had commenced his assigned task.

I needed time to let it sink in. And when it did I grew nervous and told Gitte that if only I could be directed on the use of the gadgets in the kitchen, I could go and take over the cooking from

Akobi. But I received an emphatic 'No' from Gitte. I was the visitor, she said; and for today at least the kitchen was the last place she would allow me to go. We realised, too, that we could communicate after all because Gitte spoke broken English, as I did. With the help of gestures there was no problem at all. Once this became clear to Gitte, she shouted excitedly to Akobi in the kitchen that communication was not going to be as difficult between me and her as she had thought. Gitte had barely finished speaking when Akobi rushed out of the kitchen, obviously very uncomfortable at Gitte's 'happy' news (and oh! Holy Maria! what a sight he was! Apron tied around a non-existent waist, and a big kitchen knife in one hand. Ah, if only the gods and ancestors of Naka could see this!). In our language he said to me to be very, very careful of what answers I gave Gitte with that my big mouth, because maybe he'd already given her a different answer and, please, he didn't want any contradictions!

'Why should you fear contradictions if the answers you've given her already are the truth? I won't lie,' I said.

I could see that he was fighting to keep his anger under control.

'These women,' he began, still in our language, 'these women, they are very difficult people. And that is why many times it is better not to tell them the truth. They don't understand us.'

Then grinning at a confused and suspicious-looking Gitte, who kept looking from one of us to the other with endless interruptions of: 'What did you say?' and 'What are you saying?', he said in English to her, 'I just told Mara to tell you about our marriage customs at home. The one I said I would be required to perform for you if we visit my people in Africa.'

Then, baring his teeth at me, he added, 'And you, I have told her that our father is a very big and very important chief with plenty servants and plenty hands and so on, so better take care and don't go telling her my father builds coffins for cholera victims, you hear!' And he disappeared back into the kitchen.

I smiled at Gitte, helplessly confused. Then I noticed, fortunately, that Gitte had taken Akobi at his word and discarded her suspicions, because, as soon as I turned back to her, she resumed amicably in broken English, 'When I first met your brother,

Mara, he was very lazy, a very lazy African man. At first I didn't understand, because here we hear always that African people are hard workers and love hard work because God made them specially for the hard work of the world . . .'

I winced.

'. . . but Cobby was different. So I thought, ah, this my Cobby, he is not a proper African man. But then he told me about your father who is a big chief and how, because he is an African prince, he was not allowed to work. You have plenty servants, he told me. So I tolerated it for a while. But then one day I decided that no, it can't go on like this any longer, so I confronted him. Cobby, I said to him, Cobby, you are an African prince, but here is not Africa. Here is Deutschland . . .'

I interrupted with a laugh because I was seeing in my mind's eye the true picture as it was back home: Akobi up at dawn just so he'd find a place in the public bathroom; Akobi walking to the bus stop past the public toilet and the unending heap of rubbish; Akobi in the wholesale Ministries bus! And this my Akobi was claiming to be an African prince? With plenty servants?

But poor Gitte. She misinterpreted my laughter and went on even more enthusiastically, as if anxious to gain points from me for the change she had successfully been able to bring about in her African prince. 'You don't know, Mara. Here he must work. When he is on morning shift he starts work at the mill at 4 a.m. until 12 noon. Afternoon shifts are what he likes best because then he works from 12 noon to 8 p.m. But what he hates most is the night shift, from 8 p.m. to 4 a.m. No sleep for him. So now he is living here like an ordinary labourer. And I helped him a lot to make this difficult transition, you know,' she added pompously.

Then, suddenly, she wanted to know, 'So what do you think your father would say if he heard that Cobby is living no princely life here?'

'Oh, nothing,' I stammered, with a nervous laugh. I didn't want to say anything just in case Akobi had answered the same question differently.

'Nothing?' Gitte howled. She looked disappointed, though why, I wasn't sure.

'Nothing,' I reiterated, a little more confidently, thinking that if my answer had been such a serious blunder, Akobi would by now have said something to me from the kitchen. But although it wasn't that serious, it was still a blunder.

'Ah, I don't understand,' retorted Gitte, 'why then did your brother say to me that I will have to sacrifice some cows and goats to appease your father, if he hears of it?'

'*If* he hears of it,' I said, unsure of where this would end, 'but I won't let him hear of it. And even if he hears of it, I will convince him that what you have done is good for Ako . . . eh . . . Cobby.'

Almost immediately, Akobi's voice burst furiously through from the kitchen in our language, 'O, shut that your big mouth!'

Truly, I don't have such a big mouth as Akobi is constantly saying I have.

'What did he say?' Gitte asked.

'He just thanked me for acknowledging your efforts, Gitte,' I replied.

Gitte smiled and said, 'You know, it is sad that an African prince should have to work in a factory. But you see, if he didn't, we wouldn't finish our house in time. And I want us to emigrate to Africa in two years at the latest. How far have they gone with it? Did you see it again just before you came?'

'What?'

'The house!' Gitte said.

'What house?' I frowned. And at this moment a loud crash resounded from the kitchen, interrupting us.

I rose and rushed into the kitchen. Akobi had broken four plates. I knew he had done so deliberately. He was scooping up the broken pieces when Gitte entered the kitchen.

'You don't know about the house that we are building?' she asked anxiously.

'Not the one that father built for us by the seaside, Mara,' Akobi broke in urgently. 'Gitte means the one I am building in the mountains.'

I stared foolishly at him for a moment before I grasped what he was trying to communicate to me. 'Oh, oh, that one? Oh, sorry, I didn't get it at first. That was why I got a bit confused. They have progressed fast with the foundation.'

100

This was another blunder.

'Foundation?' Gitte stammered.

'The bad ground, Gitte,' Akobi broke in again, first giving me a murderous look.

'But why didn't you tell me?' Gitte roared back.

'Because I feared that you would suggest we gave it all up, Gitte, that was why,' Akobi said desperately. 'But it's a very good place, you'll see, with beautiful surroundings, Gitte. All we need is a solid foundation, that's all.'

'Is it the weather?' Gitte queried, looking at me.

'It is the weather,' I replied, not daring to look at Akobi, 'too hot.'

And Gitte smiled, seemingly satisfied for the moment, even if not (as I could clearly see) completely convinced.

Gitte and I went back into the living room, leaving Akobi in the kitchen, his eyes streaming from the onions he was chopping. After we had sat down, Gitte remarked, 'That is why we included the swimming pool in the plan, you see.'

'Where?'

'In the house. The hot weather. Didn't you see the plan? It includes a swimming pool.'

I smiled guiltily. How could Akobi tell such big lies and put all this into Gitte's head, encouraging her to dream about the Utopia awaiting her in Africa? Swimming pool? When people were dying of hunger because they had no water for their crops? I didn't know what to say to Gitte any longer and was afraid of blundering beyond repair, so I shouted to Akobi in the kitchen, 'You must say something. I don't know what to say.'

The next second he had put his head round the door and was telling Gitte, 'That's enough now. You see what you've done? She is already complaining that you are making her talk so much when she has just arrived. It's not fair, you know. How would you like it if it's done to you, heh?'

I hated Akobi for this.

Gitte blushed deeply and turned to me. She placed her hand on mine and said, 'Entschuldigung, Mara.'

'That means sorry,' shouted Akobi.

And my heart went out to Gitte.

'And now let the spirits of our family rest a while,' he went on to Gitte. 'You have called up their names so much that they must be turning in their sleep if they are in bed, or clutching their stomachs in pain if they are having a meal.'

Later I learned that this was a strategy of Akobi's. When the going got tough he would conjure up extravagant superstitions. Gitte, who, like most Europeans, believed that all Africans were full of primitive superstitions, always fell for it.

As Osey would say, they have their own images of us: very rude, very rough, very low. We don't fight with them about these. We use them to our advantage.

13

After we had eaten – and I must say Akobi had turned into a really good cook – the question of where I would sleep arose. Since it was a two-room apartment, namely, a bedroom and a living room, it was only natural that I would sleep in the latter. When Gitte asked me whether I would prefer the couch or a mattress on the floor, Akobi shot in with lightning speed, 'Oh no, not the couch. That is out of the question. The mattress is better, more comfortable. I am sure she would prefer the mattress.'

When Gitte asked me for affirmation I said, 'Yes,' even though I knew that Akobi's hasty decision had to do not with my comfort but with his worry that I would probably dirty his couch with my big black feet. It was like his behaviour over his car. He was paranoid about the possessions that he had once dreamt about in Alhaji's corrugated-sheet house. He would stop short of nothing to protect them, even if it meant humiliating me. Once I wasn't good enough for his work colleagues to know that I was his wife. Now I wasn't good enough to have my portmanteau carried for me or sit beside him in his car. And I wasn't good enough to lay my body on his beautiful couch.

The question of why he had brought me here at all began to haunt me.

He was on night shift and was due to leave for work at 7.30 p.m. I noticed he was uncomfortable about having to leave me alone with Gitte. He kept issuing instructions and warnings to me (in our language, naturally) in the hope of averting any new blunders. 'When she asks you anything you find too risky to answer, just pretend you don't understand her broken English, you hear! And I am warning you especially about this: never answer any questions she asks about any female cousins in our family, is that clear? That is very important. You must not disobey me, Mara,' he added threateningly. 'I have brought you here to Europe, and your mother and your family must thank me for that. You too must never forget that! So don't come spoiling my stay here, or you will end up a corpse, Mara, I tell you!'

A corpse?

What he was so agitated about, naturally, was his marriage with Gitte, for if any more blunders from me should cause Gitte to discover the truth and then dissolve their marriage (which undoubtedly was what she would do if she found out) then as sure as hell the immigration would be on his heels the very next minute to put him on the next Africa-bound plane. The German immigration authorities were damned fast with the deportation of any divorced foreigner, so that he wouldn't have a chance to go wooing and marrying another German woman, and end up a legal resident again.

As soon as he had left for work I pleaded tiredness and went straight to bed on my mattress in the living room. I had also observed that Gitte had an awful lot on her chest that she wanted to let out.

Next day I was left on my own most of the time because Gitte was away at work from 8 a.m. to 5 p.m. and Akobi, after issuing me with instructions on what to cook and when to cook it, left the house without telling me where he was going. In the evening, when he went to work, Gitte left with him to go to some meeting on environmental protection.

But then came the third day and with it my next tight corner.

Akobi left for work and I was alone with Gitte for the whole evening. Pleading tiredness yet again would have betrayed to Gitte that I was trying to avoid conversation, and would rightly have made her suspicious. We watched a film together on television, a German-dubbed American film which I didn't understand but enjoyed. When it was over, Gitte went into the bedroom.

I continued watching television and would probably have gone on, just watching the pictures and understanding nothing, until close-down. But Gitte called me through to the bedroom. I went through reluctantly.

She was holding up a beautiful batik scarf, which I immediately recognised as the work of those famous traditional batik makers back home, and smiling at me. She was obviously expecting some form of reaction from me. What do I do now? I wondered, and wished that Akobi was around.

When the expected reaction was not forthcoming, she exclaimed, 'Don't you remember it?'

'That?' I asked, puzzled.

She dropped the scarf abruptly. 'You sent it to me via Osey last year when he visited home. Have you forgotten?'

'I did?'

Gitte's bewilderment turned to suspicion. 'You didn't?'

'I don't remember,' I said. 'Maybe it was another of our sisters,' I added, trying to patch up. But it didn't help much.

'Then why did Cobby say you sent it? When he told me you were coming and I asked which of his sisters it was, he replied that it was the sister who sent me the beautiful scarf. So why did he say that if it wasn't you?'

'Gitte,' I began, 'we have many sisters. Osey might have mixed us up.'

'No,' she shot back. 'What mix up? Cobby said it was you, Mara. He said your name. Mara.'

'Yes, that is why I am saying it may not be Ako . . . Cobby who made the mistake but Osey. It was Osey after all who came home and returned with the scarf for you, not Cobby.'

'I suppose you may be right,' she drawled, and slowly folded the scarf.

I left the room. I prayed to God, to this big God that my mother says is up there somewhere above the clouds and is the father of the gods of Naka and the father of the white man's God and of the gods of the Moslems and the Asians and all. I asked him to please give me the strength to see through my role. But I doubt if he heard me.

*

105

I had lived in the apartment for three weeks when, one day, Akobi called me and said that the time had come for us to think about my survival, about papers and money, and about work for me. I said I was all ears.

'There is a certain job that almost all the African women here do. But you are still a little too green for it, so we need a little more time to prepare you for it.'

'What job is that?' I asked.

'When the time comes for you to do it, I will tell you,' he said. 'Meanwhile we'll fix you up with something else while we prepare you.'

The very next week I found myself working as a housemaid for a German family. I worked three times a week and sometimes at weekends if the Madam demanded it. Akobi took the money I earned, as payment for the roof he and Gitte had provided over my head, for my food and transport, for the investment in my trip from home, and for the cost of setting me up for my coming big job.

Gitte, too, put what money she earned, from her job at the paper carton factory, into her and Akobi's joint account. From there part went on repayment of a bank loan they had taken out to buy their furniture and the car, and a larger part went towards the house being built in Africa, which I knew did not exist; which Akobi knew did not exist; but which Gitte staunchly believed existed. I couldn't tell her it did not exist, any more than I could tell her I was Akobi's wife.

I found I was slowly but surely becoming a housemaid for Akobi and Gitte, too. Before my arrival they had shared the housework. But when I arrived, I had willingly taken on some of the housework as I was at home the entire day while they were at work. Then I started the job as a housemaid. It was very hard work as there were six people in the family, among them two very untidy teenagers. During the days that I didn't go out to work for the German family I did the cleaning and ironing and cooking in the apartment.

I learnt that Akobi and Gitte took turns in making their bed, each doing four-week stints. The first three weeks that I arrived and wasn't working, it was Gitte's turn, which explains why the bed was always neatly made before they left for work. But now it was Akobi's turn, and he started leaving the bed unmade, expecting me naturally to add this task to my housework. I didn't. Never did. And this angered him.

There was a coin-operated washing machine in the block for tenants with no personal washing machine. Gitte used it to do the washing, which was the only duty that she didn't share with Akobi. She willingly put my own few clothes in too – one or two sweatshirts, and sometimes too a skirt which Vivian had sent me. Then one day I decided to strip off my jeans too and have Gitte wash them in the machine for me. Akobi saw them among the dirty pile in the washing basket. 'Can't you wash your jeans yourself?' he said. 'It's too much work for Gitte. You are used to washing clothes by hand at home, so this shouldn't be any problem for you.' I was perplexed, but I got the message.

'No,' I muttered lamely, 'it is no problem. I can wash them by hand.'

'But of course you can, Mara,' he said, and then added, tauntingly, 'Do you have golden hands? Ladies and gentlemen, here comes the African princess with the golden hands, too golden to make the bed I sleep on. Just because I sleep on it with Gitte and not with you? Oh fine, fine. But princess, hands that don't make beds must be strong enough to wash jeans.'

Gitte, who was trotting behind him, kept inquiring, 'What? What is wrong? Are you fighting?'

When she saw me remove my jeans form the washing, she said, 'I'm washing my jeans, and Cobby's too, Mara. Leave them in. Why are you taking them out?'

'Leave them in,' Akobi burst in sharply in our language. 'Didn't you hear her say to leave them in?'

To avoid any further questions from Gitte, I left the bathroom, but I knew that I wouldn't let her wash them. She was due to do the washing on Saturday afternoon. I would get up on Saturday at dawn and do my own washing. They wouldn't hear anything. They always locked the bedroom door, and besides, the bathroom was next to the living room where I slept. But at daybreak on Saturday when I took out my jeans and sweatshirts to wash, I didn't feel right about it. Gitte, after all, always did all the washing, not just hers, even if it meant just packing it into the machine. I would save her the money she would otherwise have put in the slot. And so, by the time Akobi and Gitte got up, I had done all our washing by hand. It was the precedent.

Akobi, pleased about saving a few marks, said I should always do the washing by hand. Even when I was tired or didn't feel up to it, I still did it because I felt it was expected of me. I realised, too, that Gitte wasn't all that displeased with the situation. I told myself that it was my way of compensating her for my deceit towards her. Once, when we were all three sitting in the living room, Gitte commented that it wasn't fair that I did virtually all the housework in addition to my housemaid job. Akobi retorted that she should not worry her head about it: 'Our African women work even harder than us men, Gitte. And my sister is no exception. They are brought up like that, to work, work, work. They love doing it.'

Gitte smiled gratefully at me and shrugged. So for a couple more months it continued this way, and I don't know how much longer it would have gone on, if fate hadn't struck. The events that occurred made me quite a bit less green, too.

Two things happened simultaneously. Firstly, the German family I worked for suddenly laid me off.

I went to work as usual one morning and rang the door bell, expecting Tanya, the youngest daughter, to rush to the door and open it for me as she always did. She was the one who had got used to me first and got on very well with me. But that day it wasn't Tanya at the door. It was her mother.

'Frau Mara,' she began, without even a greeting, 'I am sorry but we'll have to lay you off. I can't even let you in because I think I am being watched.'

My heart whirled.

'What have I done?' I asked. 'Didn't I do my job well?'

'Yes, yes, you did,' she replied hastily. 'Look, it's not you. Our friends on the next street, the Kohls, you know them. They were confronted yesterday by the Labour Office detectives and have been charged with employing an illegal immigrant. You know they also have an African maid, don't you? You get me now? We may be the next if we continue to keep you. So your money for

108

work done so far this month is inside your working clothes which I have put inside this plastic bag. I wish you well, Frau Mara, but I am afraid there's no more I can say or do.'

So saying, she closed the door in my face.

I don't know how I made it home in one piece. I came back to an empty apartment, as Gitte and Akobi were both at work. Not long after I had arrived the phone went. It was Vivian. She had called several times when she thought I would be alone at home. But either Akobi had answered and not given me a message, or no one had picked up the phone.

'Because I wasn't at home either, Vivian. I've been working for a German family, but as from today, no more. I've been sacked.'

'Why?' she said, astonished.

'The wife says she fears getting charged for employing me illegally,' I told her.

'Then you'll have to start the other job earlier. When are you starting it?' she asked.

'What other job?'

For a brief moment there was complete silence over the phone before she said, 'I shouldn't have asked you. I thought Akobi had already briefed you about it.' She changed the subject abruptly. 'I've got my staying papers, Mara. They gave me five years, five whole years, Mara. Can you imagine how happy I am?'

I asked about the man she had married and how much he charged her. She said he was a homosexual and had charged her a down payment of five thousand Deutschmarks, with an additional four hundred marks to be paid monthly over the next two years.

So much was happening and changing in her life, she said. Then she asked if I liked the skirt she had sent, wished me luck and then hung up, after promising to call me again.

I was alone again with my fears.

I didn't tell Gitte what had happened, when she returned from work, but I waited for Akobi, who came at 9 p.m. He listened in complete silence, then got up without a word and went straight to bed.

Now I was completely at his mercy. It wasn't long before everything I did irritated him and everything I did was wrong. I dared not smile, because . . . 'If I were you and didn't have to work but could eat three full meals a day, then I would be smiling the whole day.' And yet I dared not wear a grim face because . . . 'Ah, woman, remove that look from your face, as if you too go to work and labour eight hours a day.' I dared not walk about the apartment because . . . 'If you have nothing else to do but walk aimlessly about my apartment, then you'd better start thinking of your trip back home, Mara.' And if I sat for what, in his view, was too long at any one time, it was . . . 'Eh, woman, what is this laziness, heh? Are you not tired of sitting the whole day doing nothing?' This, when maybe I'd just finished a ton of washing – by hand, of course. Or been on my feet for hours, ironing.

When I bathed . . . 'Woman, just in case you have forgotten, water is very expensive in Germany.' And when I ironed something of mine . . . 'Just in case you don't know, Mara, it is I who pay for the electricity, not you.'

I was all muddled up. I understood the world no longer. Then something even more bizarre happened about two weeks later. Akobi announced one evening that I should be ready by 8 p.m. He was taking me out. I thought at first: No! I couldn't have heard right. I had never been anywhere outside the apartment, except to the German family's home where I had been working. But a Saturday night out with Akobi? Alone?

Then Gitte told me that because she and Cobby had been out a couple of times without me, Cobby had suggested to her that, for once, he should take me out alone, to give me a good time, he had said! And she had agreed. So, I did what I could to make myself look smart, wearing one of Akobi's shirts and a skirt and shoes belonging to Gitte. I don't know if it had to do with Gitte seeing us off in the car, but Akobi made me sit beside him in the front, for the first time ever.

Where we drove to I didn't know, but I was certain that it was outside Hamburg. Eventually we stopped in front of a gate and some bushes. Behind was a small bungalow. We walked towards it and went up three small steps to a veranda, then to the door.

Akobi pressed the bell and almost immediately a tall white man in jeans and a white T-shirt, with a large spider tattoo on his right arm, opened the door. He let us in, straight into a large living room that was dimly lit with a red lightbulb and was completely bare but for the many cushions arranged all over the floor. I did not know what in God's name could happen in a place like this, but I was with Akobi and I felt that he at least knew what he was about. And, oh yes, he certainly did.

I was told nothing. Neither Akobi nor the lanky white man said a word to me. They spoke only to each other, in German. Eventually, Akobi told me that I could sit. I slumped down onto one of the cushions while he disappeared with the lanky German into another room. Briefly, when they opened the door to the other room, I heard voices, many male voices.

Akobi returned some minutes later and brought me a glass of wine. Then I was left on my own again for a long, long while during which I finished off my wine and waited. Then something started happening to me. I was still conscious but I was losing control of myself. Something was in the wine I had drunk. It made me see double and I felt strange and happy and high . . . so high that I was certain that I could fly free. Then suddenly the room was filled with people, all men, and they were talking and laughing and drinking. And they were completely naked! There must have been at least ten men for what I saw were at least twenty images.

Then they were all around me, many hairy bodies, and they were stripping me, fondling me, playing with my body, pushing my legs apart, wide, wide apart. As for the rest of the story, I hope that the gods of Naka didn't witness it.

Next morning, when I woke up, I was on my mattress in the apartment and Gitte was teasing me about how drunk I had got the night before and how Cobby had had to carry me in here and tuck me into bed. I asked what had happened.

Gitte laughed. 'You were at a party. Have you forgotten?'

At that moment Akobi called out to her from their bedroom to please come back to bed.

Minutes later, their moaning and panting and groaning was ringing generously out from the bedroom. They were at it again.

The mattress on the living-room floor had been my bed ever since I had come to live with them. From the beginning, their lovemaking had depressed me. All sounds from the bedroom came clearly through to the living room, especially in the quietness of the night. But I had solved the problem of having to listen to it, by putting on earphones and listening to music from the cassette player. About once a month when Akobi was on the afternoon shift he had a few minutes' quick cold sex with me on the living-room floor, more, I guess, out of a sense of duty than anything else since he always first excited himself in the bedroom before coming to pounce on me and was always over with it in five minutes without having once opened his eyes to look at me. But it still hurt me when I heard him with Gitte in the bedroom making love because, even though polygamy was part of my tradition and I had been brought up to be tolerant of it, a polygamous husband back home always slept with one wife far away, out of earshot of the others. This is why African wives had their own individual huts in which they lived with their children while the husband had his own hut away from theirs, to which the wives went in turns to sleep with him. But here in this small apartment, every sound from the bedroom reached my ears.

And so this morning, suffering a cracking headache from the wine I had drunk the night before, I reached for the earphones as soon as I heard their lovemaking start. I shut my eyes and concentrated on the music when, suddenly, I felt someone rip the earphones off my head and looked up to see Akobi standing above me.

'Electricity is expensive here in Germany, Mara, just in case you didn't know.'

I was so taken aback with the unexpectedness of this action that I shouted angrily back at him, 'I know that electricity is expensive in Germany, Akobi, but I also need something to shut off all the noise that comes from you two in there,' pointing accusingly at the bedroom.

There was dead silence for a brief while. Then he stood back and stared long and hard at me, then burst into a loud laugh. He laughed so scornfully at me as if to imply, oh dear!, so you too have emotions? Just then Gitte's shrill voice interrupted us from the bedroom. 'Cobby, stop fighting with your sister. She didn't ask you to take her to the party!'

I chuckled bitterly. Ah, Gitte, she thought Akobi was fighting with me because I had supposedly got drunk at this so-called party we had attended. And I wasn't even sure what else I had drunk after that first glass of wine and whether all those naked men I thought I saw had really existed. But then, I was feeling a strange sensation between my thighs this morning, and considerable pain too. Instead of giving me any explanation about the night before, all Akobi had done was rip the earphones off my ears.

I was really angry, angry too because I was suspicious, suddenly suspicious that something else was going to happen soon. It didn't take long.

Two days later, in the afternoon, when Gitte was at work, Akobi returned unexpectedly to the apartment and with – of all people – Osey! I had spoken to him a couple of times on the telephone but hadn't seen him since I had left Vivian's apartment. And suddenly, here he was again in my life.

I was ironing when they came but I had to stop and go into the kitchen to cook because Osey said he was hungry and Akobi said I should fix him something. All the time I was cooking, Akobi sat in there on the sofa, gulping down generous measures of Russian vodka which they had brought with them. After Osey had eaten I cleared away his plates and gave him warm water and soap to wash his hands with, a napkin to dry them on and a toothpick to remove the sticky remains from between his large, long, yellow teeth. Then he called me and said there was something they had to talk with me about.

'You have now been here long enough, Mara. Have you heard of something called "Unterhaltung" before?' Osey asked me.

I hadn't, and told him so.

'It is work,' he said at last.

'So?'

'Yes. Do you want to work?' he asked slyly.

'Of course I want to work, if I can find work or if the woman I worked for before will take me back.'

Osey laughed.

'She won't take you back,' he said. 'And anyway, it's not

113

plenty money. This work that I am talking about, it is different and brings in plenty money too. Much much more plenty marks. And you will see that in a short time you will be able to make money for yourself, for your husband here who brought you over, and even be able to afford to send things home to your mother and sisters.'

'I will?' I asked cautiously. 'Then why did you let me waste all this time?'

'Because everything must come at its right time,' he answered. 'And this is the right time. You want to do it?'

'Yes.'

'Good!' He smiled. 'You are pretty. Do you know that you are pretty?'

I smiled.

He went on, 'You are pretty and you were green. Now you are no longer green. You are ripe but you are still pretty. You get me?'

'No.'

'Oh, don't worry,' he assured me with a smile, 'you will understand when the right time comes.' And he laughed. There was something about his laughter that reminded me of the time back in West Berlin when he invited me to this action film that turned out to be no John Wayne action.

The thought was worrying because, after all, didn't it fit so perfectly? You were green, now you are no longer green. When did I cease being green, and how? And when I could no longer just think about it, I asked Osey. But it was Akobi who replied.

Reeking of the vodka he'd pumped into himself, he drawled, 'But Mara, Mara, oh Mara, even if you don't want to, you will still have to. For an illegal nigger woman like you, there is no other job in Germany, Mara. If you don't get a housemaid job then there's only this. You understand? Because you are too illegal and too black for any proper job, you get it?'

Oh yes I got it, but too late, because before I could understand enough to acknowledge to myself that the best thing would be to pack my bag and flee, to return to Naka and to hawking boiled eggs, which was a far, far nobler job, I was made the property of a good-looking dark haired man who owned a sex nightclub called Peepy. How did it happen that I had let Osey and Akobi

114

drive me to this club? Why did I just stare at this man and sway, feeling that there was no way out for me and I had to do what Osey and Akobi were demanding? Why?

Before driving me to this club, Peepy, they had driven me to Osey's apartment. His wife was out. Osey had a video set, and he put in a cassette, smiling.

Osey was tough. He was a hard businessman, unscrupulous and ruthless. He didn't flinch when I began to weep. Akobi, I realised that moment for the first time, was and still is a coward. I wondered why this had never occurred to me before. All his beatings of me were the protective covering of his cowardice. But he was a greedy man. He was greedy and he was a coward, because all the time that Osey looked me straight in the face, smiling, Akobi pumped more vodka into himself in order to survive the situation.

The situation was this: the three of us were watching a video film that showed me completely naked, with men's hands moving all over my body. Then some held my two legs wide apart while one after the other, men, many men, white, black, brown, even one who looked Chinese, took turns upon me. All this was captured clearly on the video film. And this was what Osey and Akobi blackmailed me with so that I agreed to do the job at Peepy.

This world that we live in is cold. God, it is very cold. When Akobi brought Comfort to Naka and pompously showed her off, he had a dream. When Comfort gave him the showdown, his dream became more fanatical. He married me because he had a role for me in his dream. It was a dream, it seemed, he was bent on seeing through even if it meant making a sacrificial lamb of me. And so far he had got his way.

I had made the long journey from home to here. What for? I hadn't done anything for the people who helped me to come; my family, my mother. My two sons too were waiting for me. For them, too, I had done nothing. And if I could do nothing for them at all, one thing at least, I should have been left with for myself – my dignity. Now that too had been robbed of me. So was this my fate? Was this all that I was to derive from the many hens and cocks and goats whose blood had been spilled for my sake?

14

I became the responsibility of Kaye. Kaye was an African woman, too, a stunning black beauty and the wife of the good-looking man who was the owner of Peepy. Kaye was herself still partly in the trade, as we say, when time and interest allowed. But mostly she assisted her husband to manage Peepy. Not only did she polish me up splendidly to the standard of Peepy but also soon became my trusted friend when, as she herself later disclosed to me, she realised my naivety, and recognised herself in me.

She was the first person I told my whole true story, only to hear from her that she too had gone through a similar ordeal years ago, except that in her case the man who did it to her was her boyfriend and not her husband. She was surprised that a man who had formally shown his face to my family was doing this to me. And I told her of how Akobi first drowned himself in vodka before the subject of prostitution was raised with me . . .

'Even then, he was never able to look me in the face,' I added.

'Osey was the lecturer and the organiser, I can sense,' said Kaye, 'but still, for your husband to do this to you, Mara, Gitte can't be the only reason.'

'Gitte is not the reason,' I stressed to Kaye, 'his dream is the reason. Gitte is as much a victim of it as I am.'

'Still . . .' Kaye wondered, but said nothing more about it and proceeded instead to tell me about her own ordeal.

This boyfriend of hers had, like Akobi, come to Europe full of dreams. But these were shattered when he realised that the amount of money he was aiming for could take years upon years to raise. He saw how other men were making fast money with their girlfriends and so he, too, invested the little he had so far saved in bringing her from home to Frankfurt. Then he coerced her into prostitution, pocketed every mark she made and kept her in the trade by blackmailing her with pictures he had clandestinely taken of her in action with different men.

'You back out today, tomorrow these pictures will be on their way back to your family at home,' he had threatened whenever she mentioned her desire to get out of the business. So for a whole year and a half Kaye worked for him. And he took all the money she made. He said he was a music manager and bought expensive sets of instruments which he shipped home and hired out to musicians all over Africa. Then Kaye met Pompey who was now her husband. Pompey was a regular client. He told her one day that he found her fascinating and wanted to marry her. He was an up-and-coming pimp seeking to open his own sex club and could do with a beautiful black wife like her who had an understanding of his chosen trade.

'Not much of a love proposal, I know,' added Kaye, 'but at least he was honest.' She laughed. 'The boyfriend who put me in the trade, he had told me he was studying Engineering at the University. So I came believing I was coming to join my aspiring engineer husband-to-be. Yet he was waiting for me to whore for him so he could buy plenty music instrument sets and drive a Porsche and afford dinner dates with beautiful white women whose feet he would lick if they commanded him to. My people back home now have everything they want, Mara. They don't know how I make the money to buy them the things but I don't think that it even interests them very much. What matters to them is that I send them what they request. So I keep them satisfied that way and keep my peace here. And though I don't ever intend to return to them again, they don't know because I haven't told them. And I won't ever tell them. I just let them go on thinking I'll return one day. The hope alone keeps them cheerful, so I won't destroy it for them.'

'Don't they ask questions?' I asked.

'Why should they, when they get all they ask for?' Kaye replied with a trace of bitterness. 'I know one girl who used to live in Mainz, and worked as a prostitute in Mainz. The moment her family found out what she was doing here, her parents and aunts and uncles all sold what they could and bought her a ticket and insisted that she return home.'

'And she did?'

'Yes she did. She realised that her family were more interested in the maintenance of her dignity than the many things she could send them while she worked here as a prostitute. Unfortunately, not all of us have families like that. Sometimes, I think that my family suspect I'm in the trade but deliberately refrain from asking me because if they knew the truth and then took no action, not wanting to forfeit the luxuries they enjoy at my expense, they would indirectly become a party to my sins. See?'

I marvelled. 'So how long have you been married, you and Pompey?' I asked.

'Six years. And I am happy with my situation, Mara. Well . . . not happy as such. That is a lie. But I have come to terms with it. I will lead this life of mine for as long as age and health permit.'

Following this dialogue Kaye and I talked often. But the money I made laying men at Peepy, I saw none of it. Pompey was a disciplined businessman – in his field that is – who never went back on his contracts. His contract with Akobi was that from the money I made, he would deduct his percentage and deposit the rest in Akobi's private account, of which Gitte knew nothing. Here it was that my whoring profits flowed.

Every day, apart from Sundays, I took on at least three men. What they paid me went to Akobi. And Osey, too, I guess, had arranged his cut with Akobi.

I hadn't seen Gitte all this while and somehow I missed her. But I was beginning to consider this situation as my karma. I resigned myself but at the same time I began to wonder. Why couldn't I take control of my own life, since after all, I was virtually husbandless and, anyway, what did my husband care about a woman's virtue? If I was sleeping with men and charging them for it, it was me giving myself to them. The body being used and misused belonged to me. What had that got to do with

118

Akobi? So why should the money I made go to him? What had he ever done for me? Once a prostitute, always a prostitute. The stamp would never leave me. So why care about a sex orgy video with me in it? What power did he have to decide my fate in Germany? He had married and had no problem with his residency papers. He had a German wife, a home and a relatively decent life. So why did I wear myself out with men and let him take the money? If I couldn't help myself out of my situation then why not turn it to my advantage?

Initially, I kept these thoughts to myself, but one morning I made them known to Kaye. To my surprise, she exclaimed, 'At last, Mara! You have woken up. I have been waiting for you to wake up by yourself. I could have woken you up, of course, but in this business, which operates in a world of its own and is far colder than the cold world outside, it is always better to wake up by yourself. Only then do you fight to remain awake because you know how difficult that waking up has been and what a long time and a lot of thinking it takes. And you also know what it means to be asleep. You understand?'

'No,' I answered with a smile.

'It means you were a fool and now you are less a fool. Get me?'

We both laughed.

But, as I said, Pompey was a rigidly disciplined businessman, and Kaye knew he wouldn't fall in with any deal to help me behind Akobi's back. We had to plan carefully.

'Mara thinks she should go easy and just have one a day, Pee, for the next three months or so,' she told her husband sweetly one morning. Pee was her pet name for her husband.

'She's been destroyed down there, Pee,' she replied when Pompey asked why. 'It was that Italian who came to see her for the first time yesterday. He almost completely destroyed her, Pee. I think her decision is wise. After all, that's her capital and she must take care not to lose it, which is what will happen if she doesn't slow down, Pee.'

Pompey eventually agreed.

Our plan was put into motion. I didn't reduce my daily customers to one as Kaye had told Pompey. I increased them to seven. It wasn't without risks of course, but with the experienced

Kaye as my accomplice, all risks were worth taking and seemed conquerable.

Kaye, as I said before, was still in the trade when time and interest allowed. During this period, rather than turn her customers away when for one reason or the other she couldn't serve them, she passed them secretly on to me. There were others, too, whom she privately contacted, some who came to my room in Peepy when Pompey was away, and others whom I dated with Kaye's help and met for one or two hours at hotels. Kaye explained my many movements in and out of Peepy as visits to a certain Turkish woman who was relieving my genital pains, using a herbal treatment.

Taking on seven men a day was crucifying but I was aiming for a certain amount of money, plenty money, and the sooner I raised it the better, since the longer the time, the greater the danger of Pompey finding me out.

When I wasn't sleeping with a man I was crouching over a bucket of steaming hot water diluted with camphor and alum. Sometimes the treatment left me with a numb vagina, so that I even felt nothing when the men were sleeping with me, but it was better than the pain. On top of it all, I was swallowing scores of pain killers and tranquillisers every day and taking drugs to keep me going. Only when I had my period did I get some rest. But even before five weeks was up I was ready with my cash to pay some German guy to marry me, so that I could get my resident papers.

I was impressed how quickly and smoothly these arrangements could be made if one had the cash and the right contacts. I didn't even need to leave Germany as many people do. Only my passport left Germany, with the German guy Kaye had arranged for me to marry. An African or Caribbean woman living in Copenhagen, who looked a bit like me, took my place at the registry office and forged my signature. The German guy came back with a marriage certificate that said we were man and wife. He had received half his fee before going to Copenhagen. Back in Germany, when all the visits to the Foreign Office had been made and the countless forms had been filled in, and I eventually got the blessed stamp of a five-year resident's visa in my passport, he received the other half of his money. In addition, I was to pay him two hundred Deutschmarks a month for the next two years. But I could afford it.

All this happened over a period of about three months. Neither Akobi nor Osey knew anything about it.

Initially when they had brought me to Peepy and handed me over to Pompey, one or other – more often Osey – would phone at least once a week to ask how I was doing. Only once did they come to visit me and even then they didn't stay for more than ten minutes. But once the money I had begun making started flowing into their bank accounts, even the telephone calls ceased. So what had become of them, I didn't know; just as they, too, didn't know what had become of me. Then one day, having resigned myself to my karma (what will be will be), and feeling confident about myself because of my new resident status, I picked up the telephone and called Gitte and made a date with her at an ice-cream parlour. I knew that I was intending something which had to do with Akobi but what it was was still a muddle in my mind. Gitte, I decided, might help me focus.

'Mara!' Gitte screamed down the phone, on hearing my voice. I told her it was crucial that Akobi heard nothing about the call and our plan to meet because I had had a fight with him and he had forbidden me to see his wife. So Gitte must have known what she was doing when she suggested this obscure Italian ice parlour.

She was really excited to see me and we embraced warmly. I wanted to know everything that had happened to her over the past half-year and she wanted to know all my news. I lied that I was living with some relatives outside Hamburg and that I was working as a housemaid again for a German family. While we ate our ices, I prepared myself for my inquiries.

I had a strong suspicion, instinct perhaps. I guess it had been there a long while now, subconsciously, maybe even since I had come to join Akobi and found him still treating me like the foolish little village girl from Naka. Or maybe, too, it started seeping into my consciousness when Kaye had flatly stated that it couldn't be because of Gitte alone that Akobi was treating me this way. I don't know. But it was there. And it was waiting for the right moment to surface. I was able to confront it when my stay no longer depended on Akobi's deals and so-called useful connections, when I realised that I could now do without him.

'Gitte,' I began. My palms were sweating, 'Gitte, do you know any relative or friend or . . . or . . . someone that Ako . . . Cobby knows who is called Comfort?' I asked eventually.

'Your cousin?' Gitte asked snappily. It was at once evident that all was not rosy between her and this our supposed cousin, Comfort.

Suddenly I ceased sweating. It was the fear and anxiety that I wouldn't get this answer that had made me sweat. This was the answer I had been waiting and hoping for. Now that I had it, the worst was over. All I needed now was to find out more about this my cousin Comfort.

'You know her well?' I asked Gitte.

'Oh yes,' she replied disdainfully, with a frown.

I needed a description of this Comfort that Gitte knew, to see if it would tally with Mama Kiosk's description of the Ministries girl Comfort whom Akobi had spent his final important days with before leaving home. This woman who had once snubbed him but who smiled back at him when she heard he was preparing to travel to Europe.

'What does she look like?' I asked.

'Tall,' replied Gitte, 'she is tall and not as black as you. More like brown. She has lots of hair, too. And very beautiful big eyes.'

'That's our cousin,' I confirmed. 'So she is here?'

'Yes,' Gitte sounded a little surprised. 'Didn't you know? She came last year' (this was Gitte's way of saying 'two years ago'), 'with Osey, when he was returning from Africa, after that visit when he brought me your . . . the scarf.'

I don't know why, but this news affected me badly. Akobi, as a person, no longer affected me. But his manipulation of the situation made my heart pound. I went hot and cold, and felt faint. After a few moments I recovered.

'I see,' I muttered. But Gitte had become suspicious, having observed my reaction, so I had to come up with some excuse.

'I just don't understand my brother, Gitte,' I lied. 'How could he ask his cousin to come and join him before his sister? Can you understand that?'

'Please,' urged Gitte, to my surprise, 'don't go and fight with him about this, Mara, I beg you. Because otherwise he will be very angry with me, you see. I don't want trouble again. We already had a very big problem about her before you came, you know.'

'You did?'

'Yes,' Gitte replied, 'a very big problem, Mara. And I am very sorry to tell you this, Mara, because you are her cousin, but I don't like her. I didn't like her before and I still don't like her.'

'Because she is our cousin?' I asked.

'No,' she replied haltingly, 'not that exactly, but something like that. You see, even though Cobby said they were cousins, it was like they were not proper cousins. I got the feeling that . . . that . . . ah Mara . . .'

'That what?' I pressed.

'Oh, Mara, please, you must not be angry that I talk like this about your cousin.'

'No, I won't be angry,' I replied hastily. 'You talk,' I urged her.

'Well, I don't know what made me think this way, Mara. I know it may be stupid or maybe even over-reacting. But every time I came in from outside, especially from work, and saw them together, I had this feeling that they had been sleeping together.'

'Why?' I asked.

'You see, she was not like you, Mara. Although she was not a natural beauty like you, she was very attractive. So I think, too, that I was afraid. She was different, Mara, different and . . . let me see . . . sophisticated. That was it. And you know, some cousins can love each other. And that was the thought that gave me the fear. You understand?'

I didn't reply.

'I love your brother, Mara,' Gitte resumed softly, as if she was about to cry. 'And it is my love for him that has now left me without a family, Mara. My family didn't want me to marry a foreigner, and worse still, a Negro, you understand? They said that if I married him they would have nothing more to do with me. And they have kept their word, Mara. The only one who sees me is Franz, my little brother, and even then, secretly. As

123

for my father, when he heard that I had married a Negro, he started to drink. Now he drinks so much and beats my mother, blaming her for not bringing me up properly. So you see, Cobby is really all I have left. Which is why I am always so afraid of losing him, you see.'

'And why were you not afraid of me as you were of Comfort?'

'Because you are his sister and not his cousin. Cousins are much more likely to sleep together than a sister and brother. And you were different . . . simple, not sophisticated like Comfort. I noticed too that Cobby has power over you. He controls you. It wasn't like that with Comfort at all. She had the power. She controls Cobby and shouts at him. Then, too, with Comfort, Cobby wanted a different arrangement . . . and at our expense. He didn't want her to live in the apartment with us like you did because he said that Comfort would tell your family that we made her sleep on a couch in the living room while we slept comfortably on a bed in the bedroom. And that would anger your father so much that when we went to Africa your people wouldn't be nice to me.'

'And where did he want her to live?'

'In her own apartment. He wanted to rent a whole apartment for her in town. I didn't like it because it was expensive, you see. He was expecting that we would pay the rent and bills for her till she could afford to pay them herself. But we needed money as much then as we do now, to finish our house in Africa. I told Cobby that but he still insisted that he wouldn't have Comfort living with us and sleeping in the living room like she was our housemaid.'

'He said that?'

'Yes. So there was big trouble. You see, Mara, I want to leave here. I want to leave Germany with Cobby, to go and live forever in the sun in Africa, in our house. That is why I want us to finish it quickly. Here, I am fed up. They call me "Negerweib" everywhere. Even in the factory where I work. And many times too when I must go and do something that involves administration and paperwork, I must hear over and over again, oh, you are married to a foreigner? Ah, a Negro too? I am tired of it, Mara. I want us to work hard together and to finish our house

124

so that we can leave this country behind us once and for all. So now you understand why I wasn't happy when you said that only the foundations of our house had been laid?'

I sat there and said nothing. I was shocked, angry and bitter. I was filled with pity for myself, but even more so for Gitte.

'You see,' she resumed when she saw that I wasn't going to talk, 'I want us to finish the house quickly so that we can go and live there before I grow too old to have children. I want about four.'

'And Cobby? How many does he want? Has he said?'

Gitte laughed.

'He says always that he wants at least eight. Oh, but he is crazy. He was only joking.'

'A German man may be joking when he says that but not an African man, Gitte,' I said.

We laughed together.

I wanted very much to ask Gitte if Akobi had ever told her that he had a child but I couldn't find a way of saying this without shocking and upsetting Gitte. And anyway, who would I say was the mother?

'You know why I was angry the first day you came and I arrived home to find you?' Gitte was saying.

'No,' I answered.

'Comfort,' she said, 'because of Comfort. I thought that it was going to start all over again with us as it did with Comfort. And that was terrible, I tell you, Mara. He had more time for Comfort than he had for me. He took her all over the place. "This is an all-African affair, Gitte," he would say when he was going somewhere with her and leaving me behind. "You would be the odd one out, Gitte." And then he would stay out very late, too. Afterwards I would hear that not only did he go with Comfort to her place after the occasion but also that it wasn't an all-African affair, that other African men had come with their German wives and girlfriends. So he could have taken me along. That was why I was very angry the day you arrived at the apartment. Because when he went to collect you he forgot to come and pick me up in time. And I thought to myself, now Comfort has gone, Mara has come . . .'

'Comfort has gone?' I interrupted.

'No. Ah, I don't know. Maybe she has gone or maybe she is still here. I can't tell for sure. But now Cobby has come to his senses about her after I threatened him with divorce. I even moved out of the apartment for a week. But he came and pleaded with me and promised me that it would be different with Comfort from now on. That is why we are still together today.'

My heart was pained inside me. It was pained inside me for my own self and for Gitte, too. My situation was bad enough but hers was worse still because at least I knew the truth about what I was to Akobi. Here was Gitte at loggerheads with her family because of this same Akobi, who did nothing but cheat on her.

'Did Cobby pay for her to come? I mean Comfort?' I asked eventually.

'Yes. But don't tell Cobby I told you this, okay?'

'I won't,' I assured her. 'I told you I've fought with him and I'm no longer speaking with him. But why does it worry you?'

'Because, Mara, Cobby says if I tell anyone that he paid for Comfort to come and we go to Africa your people won't be nice to me because they will say that . . .'

I wasn't going to hear any more of that tale.

'I'll have to be going, Gitte,' I interrupted.

'Oh! So suddenly? But Mara, you haven't even finished your ice,' she protested.

'I truly must be going, Gitte,' I insisted, 'but I'll call you again, okay? And we can make another date.'

We were both weeping. I'm not sure that either of us knew why.

'You promise to call?' she said.

'I promise,' I said, and managed a laugh.

Before I left, Gitte took out her handkerchief.

'Here, take this,' she said. 'Then we'll have to meet again, so that you can give it back to me.'

15

'Mara, Pee is still paying money into your husband's account, you know,' Kaye told me one evening at the bar at Peepy when we were alone.

'Let him,' I replied.

'And what will you do now that you've got your papers? You know you can even travel to Africa and return to Germany straight through Frankfurt, without any problems, because of your five-years visa?'

'I know, Kaye,' I replied.

She looked quizzically at me and said, 'You need a new name, Mara.'

It was my turn to be surprised. 'Do you have anything against the name Mara?' I asked.

'No. It's a beautiful name,' she said, 'but Mara is no more.'

'Where is she?' I asked ironically.

'She is standing before me,' answered Kaye, 'but she isn't the same any more. You are no more you, Mara. You've changed.'

'No, Kaye,' I said, 'I'm still me. I have just understood the world a bit better.'

I had been wanting to get Vivian's number for a while now. Eventually I got Kaye to call Osey's home when I knew he wouldn't be there. She talked to his German wife, pretending to be an old friend of Vivian's who had just arrived in Berlin. Osey's wife gave us a Stuttgart number. The woman who answered the phone said we could leave our number and she would give it to Vivian next time she turned up, which was not very often.

Two weeks later, Vivian called me. She was excited and high. I wanted to know where she had been and how come no-one knew her contact number.

'I have disappeared, Mara,' she said.

'I beg your pardon?'

'I've gone.'

'Where? What do you mean?'

'From Osey, Mara. Far, far gone! Direction America. Land of yankees and steaks, here I come. Take me whole, Lady Liberty. I love the sons of your womb!' She laughed loudly.

'Vivian, are you feeling all right?' I asked, genuinely concerned.

'Do I feel all right? Of course! What do you think? I am okay, Mara. And that is why I butted Osey deep in the arse! Do you know that he beat me up with the pressing iron?'

'Why, Vivian, why did he do that?'

'Because I went shagging with a GI. Soldier my love . . . soldier my love . . . take me in your arms . . .' she started singing tunelessly, then stopped abruptly and said, 'Mara, do you know something?'

'What?' I asked.

'I'm in love, Mara,' she said, 'with a GI.'

'Who is GI?' I asked.

'Marvin,' she replied. 'He is a GI.'

'What is GI?' I asked.

'Government Issue, capital letters. American soldier based in Wiesbaden. Soldier love. Ah Mara, I love him. I love him so much that I bought him a gold chain. And then kicked Osey in the arse.'

'With Marvin's soldier boots?'

We both laughed.

'But why did you want to talk to me, Mara?' Vivian suddenly asked.

I remained silent.

'Mara, are you there?'

I decided to be straightforward. 'I want you to tell me what you know about Comfort, Vivian.'

There was a long silence. Then she said, 'Oh my God, Mara, so you've found out?'

'I have.'

'Oh my God!' she muttered again.

'Did you know it all along? From the time I came?' I asked her.

'I did,' she admitted.

'And you put on all that show? Convincing me to be tolerant and do what you were all telling me?'

'You were green then, Mara. Totally green. And I was also in love with Osey then. And I did what Osey ordered me to do. I was his property then, Mara. I loved him, Mara. I really did.' Her voice trailed off.

'What's wrong, Vivian?' I shouted. 'I'm not blaming you! I just need information.'

'It's not you, Mara,' she sniffed.

Another long silence. Then suddenly, 'You know what, Mara? Ingrid is pregnant.'

'Who is Ingrid?' I asked.

'Osey's wife. His German wife. Can you understand that, Mara? I am his first wife. He didn't make a child with me, but went and made a baby with Ingrid. Can you understand that? I was always telling him, we must make a child, Osey, we must make a child and send it home. And what did he tell me? Wait! Always, wait, wait, wait. And before I knew what was happening, Ingrid was pregnant.'

It was my turn to be shocked.

'I thought he said he married her for convenience?' I said.

'Which doesn't mean they don't sleep together,' she answered. 'And you know what is even worse? Ingrid asked if I could come and live with them when her baby arrived and help her take care of it. I said, "Ah, Ingrid, but you don't have a big enough apartment," and she said, "Not to worry, Vivian. Osey said we are taking on a new apartment, a bigger one. Four rooms." And I said, "But that is expensive, Ingrid." And she said, "But Osey says he can afford the payments." And why do you think he can afford the rent, Mara? Because I was there, Mara. I was there to work for him.'

129

'So what did you tell Ingrid?' I asked.

'I told her I was sorry, but that by then maybe I would be carrying my own baby too, somewhere in Chicago.'

'Is Marvin in Chicago?' I asked.

'Marvin is here. When he leaves here at the end of his service he goes to Chicago.'

'And you'll go with him?'

'He can't go without me. He's got a big taste for hashish and needs at least four rolls every month. You think his soldier pay can finance that? Only a whore's income can finance that. Hey, but I'm happy, you know!'

She sounded very far from happy.

'I got Marvin,' she went on, 'I got my papers, I got hashish and I got a profession that I can practise in every corner of the world. Can you give me a better formula for happiness?'

'Vivian, I said I called about Comfort. Where is she now?'

'I'm not sure,' she said, 'but I once heard she was working as a waitress in an Afro-Caribbean restaurant in Hanover or somewhere.'

'Is that all you know?'

'Yes.'

'Why don't you give me your number so I can call you when I need to talk to you?' I asked.

'No.'

'And how do I get you again?'

'Like this time. Call that couple in Stuttgart. Tell them you want to talk to me. They will tell me when I call them. Even they don't know my number.'

'Are you in hiding because of Osey?' I asked her.

'Because of everything and everyone, Mara. Everything.'

The line clicked. She was gone.

'Now I am ready to listen to you, Kaye,' I said when I returned to her.

'What about?' she asked.

'About how you can help me out of my situation.'

'What situation?' she asked.

130

'I don't want Pee to continue paying my money to my husband,' I said.

'Then I'll have to think up something,' she said. 'You need money?'

'I've got plenty of it under my mattress. You know that. I'm just ready to provoke now. You know a good private detective?'

'If you are prepared to be quite generous.'

'I am,' I said.

Seeing the determination on my face, Kaye added, 'Well, I've told you about the other channels, Mara. Those films, they pay enormously. And you are so beautiful that I am sure many will clamour for you. Pee can also fix you up for shows, you know, if you are serious about it. Stage shows.'

I turned and faced Kaye and said, 'Kaye, I came here to you and Pee and all the others with thick bushy hair which has now been exotically cut short, close to my scalp. My eyebrows have been plucked thin. I have mastered the use of make-up, so that my lips are never without their scarlet taint. And I have received into me the rigid tools of many men and accompanied them on sinful rides through the back doors of heaven and returned with them back to earth, spent men. I am no longer green and you know it. As for the morals of life my mother brought me up by, I have cemented them with coal tar in my conscience. If the gods of Naka intended me to live by them, they should have made sure I was married to a man who loved me and who appreciated the values I was brought up with. I lived by these values until I could no longer do so. The rot has gone too deep for me to return to the old me. And that is why, Kaye, I am going to do the films and the stage shows and all there is to it. But I want every pfennig of what I make to come to me!'

'Pee won't agree to it unless you agree to let him sit down and sort it out with you, your husband and Osey. You know how he is.'

'I know,' I said. 'That's why I'm not going to start yet with the films and stage and what else shows. The day I know every pfennig I earn will come to me, that is when I will start.'

Kaye shook her head slowly in wonderment. Then she wrote

something on a piece of paper and gave it to me. It was the address of a private detective.

Three days later I found my way to the address Kaye had given me. The office, if it could be called an office, was situated in the cellar of an apartment block and furnished with just a table, a chair and an armchair.

'For my clients,' he said, pointing to the armchair with a smile.

'And if there are two of them?' I asked.

'Then I give them my chair and I sit on the table,' he replied with a laugh.

The ice was broken between me and Gerhardt Strauss, private detective for all cases.

'How do you get your clients? Do you advertise yourself or something?' I wanted to know.

'No. Through contacts,' he replied, 'personal contacts. That is what makes me exclusive, because as you see,' he waved his hands about the room – 'this is far from what you call exclusive.'

I laughed with him. He walked back to his chair and sat down behind the table. I sat in the armchair facing him.

'We can now begin,' he said unexpectedly, rather formally. But it did help me to begin.

'I want to know all about an African woman here in Germany. The last anyone heard of her, about a year ago, she was a waitress at an Afro-Caribbean restaurant in Hanover.'

'That shouldn't be difficult. There aren't many Afro-Caribbean restaurants in Hanover,' he said. 'What's her name?'

'I only know her first name. Comfort.'

'Description?'

'Tall. Brown. Big, beautiful eyes. Sophisticated. And if she hasn't cut her hair, then plenty hair. And then a man, too. Akobi. He now calls himself Cobby. That's the first name. Second name is Ajaman. He is married to a German woman called Gitte who works at a carton factory. She is short, fat, auburn and not pretty. Lives with him in Scharlemann Strasse 54.'

'Anything precisely you want to know?' he asked.

'Everything,' I said. 'Everything about them. Especially Comfort and Akobi. If Gitte has to come in, no problem, just so long as it won't bring pain or discomfort to her. I want to know especially about Cobby's activities since he's been living here in Germany.'

'In Africa, too?'

'Yes. Even if it means someone having to travel there,' I said. 'I'll pay.'

'What do you want to know about his activities?'

'His financial deals, private arrangements, properties acquired, if any. Every deal and activity that you are capable of finding out about, I want to know.'

'I am capable of finding out about everything,' he said formally.

'I want to know about anything involving him and Comfort, or him and Gitte, or all three. All that he's done and is doing. All that he's achieved and is achieving and how he achieved these things. His intentions . . .'

'Even the colour of his toilet paper?' He laughed.

'Yes, even the colour of his toilet paper,' I replied, also with a laugh. 'When should I expect my first news.'

'When I tell you I'm ready,' he replied, 'Kaye will let you know.'

I left his place feeling very encouraged. Kaye was waiting for me when I returned to Peepy.

'I have worked out what you should do, Mara,' she said. We were in my room where I was preparing for a customer who had called to say he would be there in an hour. One of the few who always made an appointment first. Maybe it had to do with his profession by day: he was a respectable lawyer who worked for a well-known firm, and by night a whore-payer.

'About my situation?' I asked her.

'Yes. Mara, if you want to make a new start without confrontations and troubles with your husband or Osey, and since Pee is too rigid to bend, a new town, a new brothel and a new lord are your answer.' ('Lord' was Kaye's word for pimp.)

'Frying pan into fire?'

'Vice versa,' said Kaye, 'let's say, fire into frying pan.'

'Both burn,' I said. 'Is there a difference?'

'I don't know,' Kaye replied, 'but at the moment you have little choice.'

A brief silence elapsed, then I said, 'It means I'll be leaving you, Kaye.'

'I know,' she said.

'And I don't know if I'll like it,' I said.

'Changes can be necessary,' said Kaye. 'And they sometimes involve risks and pain and compromise. The plan I have for you will get you out of here. Listen. You now have a recognised status and you can move freely and work in any part of Germany. So I suggest that you leave Hamburg altogether. Move afresh to the south. To Munich.'

'That's very far away,' I said.

'So much the better,' Kaye replied. 'There is this guy there, one of the best in his field. And just as disciplined as Pee once he agrees to a deal. I'll tell him the whole truth of your story and he will know how to hold your husband and Osey at bay. You'll find him a good lord just so long as you don't try to cheat him or to wriggle a smart arse at him. In other words, Mara, whatever deal we come to, stick to it.'

'And where will Pee come in?' I wanted to know.

He won't,' replied Kaye. 'This man is my friend, not his or ours.'

'How will I leave here without Pee knowing?'

'You will escape.'

'How?'

'You and I and the others will leave as usual for Schroeder's.' (Dr Schroeder was our gynaecologist to whom we went every fortnight for a check-up.) 'Then as usual, from Schroeder's we will go shopping. We will part and go our separate ways as usual, with an agreed time to meet at the car. We will all be there, except you. You simply won't turn up.'

'And where will I be?'

'On a Munich-bound train. Oves will be expecting you. He is your new lord.'

'And what will you tell Pee?'

'That I suspect you've run away to Holland.'

'Hm,' I sighed. 'Well planned, Kaye.'

'Down to the minutest detail,' she said with a smile.

'And what is his cut of my income?' I asked.

'Oves? Thirty.'